Namik Dokle, journalist, dramaturge, prose writer.

He is the author of several collections of short stories, some of which have been incorporated in various anthologies. However, as the author of three collections with plays, he is better known as a playwright. In fact, eight of his fourteen plays have been successfully staged and performed for long periods in the theaters of the country. Dokle has also been awarded national and international prizes for some of them. Additionally, his six radio dramas have all been performed on Radio Tirana.

Yet, in recent years, his literary contribution has mostly been in the genre of the novel. He has already published four: *Vajzat e mjegulles* (*The Girls of Fog*), *Lulet e skajbotes* (*The Flowers of World's Edge*), *Ditet e lakuriqeve te nates* (*The Days of the Bats*), *Kolerë në kohë të dashurisë* (*Cholera in the Time of Love*). Dokle's novels have also been translated and have attained significant success in Bosnian, Turkish, Bulgarian and Spanish languages.

To Mother,
More so than to anyone else.

Namik Dokle

THE GIRLS OF FOG

TRANSLATED FROM THE ORIGINAL
BY EDONA LLUKAÇAJ

AUSTIN MACAULEY PUBLISHERS™

LONDON * CAMBRIDGE * NEW YORK * SHARJAH

A CIP catalogue record for this title is available from the British Library.

ISBN 9781035810246 (Paperback)
ISBN 9781035810253 (ePub e-book)

www.austinmacauley.com

First Published 2023
Austin Macauley Publishers Ltd®
1 Canada Square
Canary Wharf
London
E14 5AA

Jesene mëgle panale
Putnicam putoj kazhujet…
The fallen fogs of autumn,
Show the path to travellers …
(Gorani song)

Part One

1

Even today, after fifty-seven years have passed by, that wild, sad and vengeful wail that slashed the night in two and made heaven and earth into one whirls throughout my whole being. The stars went out instantly and I was left alone in the darkness, trembling from something that went beyond horror. I was dreaming that cold winter morning, when the day was still afraid of to break: a strange dream that had sent chills down my spine, even though I was near a burning fire. I touched the flames with my hands, I approached, but the closer I got, the colder I felt. I thrust myself into the fire, yet, still nothing: only the chill. The moment I was enveloped by the cold fire, I heard that wail I couldn't trace.

Was it coming from the ground or from the sky? I went out to the porch, right when all the stars went out for fear of that piercing scream and I was shaking, confused as to where the door of the room had gone. 'Get in! Quickly!' Father told me and pulled me like a sack of wet grass. Mother tucked me in bed with care, but I could not escape the chills that followed through my body, to the inside of my chest.

'What was it?' Mother asked.

'The bears,' Father said. 'They are mourning the murdered mother…calamity will befall this village that killed the bear.'

These words shook me even more than the howl of the orphaned bears did. They had already ceased, or had penetrated deep into the beech, but their wail still lingered inside me and, I don't know why, but it felt as if my eyeballs were going to jump out of their sockets and burst on the ground. Father grabbed the scissors with which we sheared the sheep, and left the house half-dressed. I grabbed Mother's hands and was afraid to let them go until Father was back. He handed Mother something small and black, the size of the finger of a new-born baby, and in a hoarse voice told her: 'Make a *bazibén*[1] with this.'

'What, what is it?'

'The bear's claw,' Father said. 'Sew it in cloth and hang it on his *mitan*[2]. His fear of the bear will disappear. It was the last claw; the others got scared before us and took them all.'

'Is she still there?' Mother asked.

'Still there. But today they will take her away, because she has started to smell.'

The bear had been killed by the border guards three days earlier.

A scaffold with beech logs had been erected in the square in front of the Burnt Mosque. That's where they had placed the bear. The entire village had rushed to see it. Many women had even forgotten to wear their black veils out of haste. People from the other neighbourhoods had come as well, and the following day, so did people from the villages around. I went several times and the dark nails and frozen eyes, which had no whites like the eyes of humans do, were carved onto my retina. Those who went there did not speak, they only shook their heads thoughtfully, and left; perhaps they too believed that after killing the bear, calamity would befall our village. 'Who killed it? Where was it killed?' they would ask. And whoever happened to be nearby would briefly respond: 'At the border.'

The soldiers who shot her stayed there for a few hours, but only on the first day, when they dragged it to the middle of the village with the help of a horse. The second day, the women and girls did not come to fetch water at Topillo, the fountain with the best water in the village, as it flowed just a few steps away from the victim's scaffold. A friend of mine took a stone from the rubble of the Burnt Mosque and flung it in the direction of the bear. But one of the men picked up the stone which had fallen on her hind legs and, throwing it back into the rubble with a frown, said: 'You can't hit with the stones of the mosque.'

The howl of the orphaned bears was only heard on the third night. 'Maybe they smelled their mother just now,' Mother said, without looking at either me or Father. She took care to cover my shoulders a bit more and, in a tired voice, she added she would wake me up to go to the mill. 'There is no more flour left,'

---

[1] Amulet

[2] A vest like article of clothing with detached sleeves

she justified. The howling of the bears continued till the dawn of that foggy and cold day.

2

Even I had come to notice that there was no more flour in the pantry and we were forced to—as the saying goes—even eat unripe squash and their seeds. The day before, Father had sent me to Mursel, in Orgosta, without saying a single word. He gave me almost no instructions at all. Go and ask where his house is. Only that. It would be my first time going there, by the river that flowed from Kosovo, somewhere near the Sharr Mountains. It was only when I entered the forest that I became frightened and began to sing out loud to defeat the ill-omened envelopment of beeches. I heard no wolves or bears howling, but my heart skipped a couple of beats when rabbits hopped from one side of the path to cross to the other.

'Rabbits crossed my path, it's bad luck,' I told Mursel when I found his house.

'No, do not worry, the rabbit is light and not bad luck.'

He did not inquire about my visit at all.

'Father sent me,' I told him, but he did not respond. Then he put some wood to the fire and told me to move closer. The heat of the burning coal melted my fear away.

'You have gotten more chills from fear than you have from the winter cold,' he told me. I do not know how long I stayed there, warming up, and how many more times I asked myself why I was there at all. Mursel, a calm man, with a short beard and a tear constantly on his eyelids because of the fireplace smoke, would come and go, smoking his pipe, and rarely speaking a word. When I least expected it, one of the brides of the house, a tall girthy woman entered the room and placed a dining table near my feet. She left and returned with a pan of corn *peta*[3], emitting steam that smelled of pickled cabbage. 'You and

---

[3] A dish similar to noodles

I will eat now, because the others are at work,' Mursel said as he approached the table.

So this is why Father sent me, I thought to myself. *Hunger had started to reign in our house days ago.* The land we owned on the mountain slope and the stony tract below did not suffice to feed us. Nor did the rations that the state would occasionally distribute among the villages. The previous years, Father would go to Has to tinker the dishes, and he would bring grain and other food from there, but over the past two years neither him, nor his friends dared to go on this trip. 'Better to die from hunger than from lice,' Mother would say.

Three years ago, one of the tinsmiths was struck by typhus and their house was sealed off for several weeks. We too were overcome by fear. What if Father were to catch it? During the day, I passed by the house sealed with planks and nails to learn how the people inside were doing; whether any had died; whether the planks had been pulled out of the windows and doors. Though, at night, I dreamt of lice and woke up terrified. The worst of those nightmares—which is probably why I remember it to this day—was the one in which I would go to graze the sheep in the mountains, but they would turn into black lice, as big as the sheep themselves, and destroy the mountain altogether.

'Eat, eat,' Mursel kept urging me, assuming that I was reluctant to eat in a foreign house, while, in fact, it was the black sheep that haunted me. But I soon forgot about them and my mouth was filled with the flavour of corn and pickles. Although silently, I would constantly whole-heartedly thank the good Mursel, the beautiful bride who brought the table and the pan of *peta*, which she must have baked herself, Father who sent me to this small village to satiate and warm my stomach, wrinkled from the hunger which had befallen our house. When both of us, Mursel and I, were full, there was still food left in the pan. What if I asked to take them to Mother?

'Now you can go,' Mursel told me. I climbed down the wooden stairs and saw our mule loaded not only with a small sack of grain but also with two wicker baskets woven with hazelnut twigs, stuffed with unshucked corn. Good-hearted Mursel! Father had sent me to get grain, and he distracted me with little talk until the *peta* were baked. He did not step down, but greeted me from the stairwell on the second floor of the house, shouting behind me: 'Don't be scared of rabbits!'

I tried to gather a little courage, but it would quickly evaporate, when all the sorts of stories came to my mind: those of people who ran through the winters to scavenge for some food to take home, but who would, at times, get torn apart by

15

wolves, killed by thieves or runaways, or even caught by a storm and then found frozen seven days later. And even if they had managed to escape the dangers, they would return home to find their children starved because of the delay. This was also the case of a woman in our village, who had found her two sons dead. Every day, she would take food to their graves, and after weeping and screaming, she would stutter: 'Eat my dears, eat before the food gets cold!'

3

When I headed for the mill, I had to pass by the killed bear once again. *'I will probably not be seeing her when I get back,'* I thought to myself, *'by then, they will have removed it.'*

'Now that we killed the bear, the lice will meet their end. We will kill them with the bear,' had been the words of Salko, a villager from the lower neighbourhood, the only redhead in our village. He then revealed that the Organisation had decided to turn the bear's fat into soap in order to protect the village from the ever-present threat of lice. In fact, only a handful of houses had gotten lice, but that had been enough to terrify the rest of us. At school, they had once removed a boy's white cap, only to count eleven black bugs crawling freely and unbothered, like the *seymens*[4] of the past.

Even though I passed quite close to the bear, I could not smell the rot, probably because one of the bags loaded onto the mule was filled with roasted oats which had a prominent aroma. We used oats for cattle or to catch quails, deceiving them with its strong scent. It would be our first time that we used oat for bread, after mixing it with Mursel's corn. This was the only way we would perhaps get by until the barley ripened in Vlahanica, the field that our grandmother had passed on to us three years ago, when typhus struck the tinsmith's house.

'You're all going to neigh,' the miller told me as he unloaded our grain. I leered at him. He was known as a man that seldom said a word. The mill was down by the river and, partially from the deafening sound of the mill and partially because he had never had time to mingle with the men, he seemed to have forgotten to speak. Even the mother that gave him birth had provided him with a pair of lips that were always half open and this made the miller look as if he was always silently speaking. Quite often, when he was in the company of others,

---

[4] A military rank introduced by the Seljuk and also present in the Ottoman Empire

they would ask him: 'Did you say anything?' and he would shrug: 'No, I didn't.' And now, he seems to have learned how to speak and dares to tell me: 'You are all going to neigh.'

'The oats will also be damaging the millstone, but what can I do,' he said, emptying the oats into the hopper. 'At a time when people have nothing to eat, why am I worrying about the millstone?' I had never heard him say so many words in my entire life.

As we were loading the flour, a man from the Locality brought grain to grind. 'Our millstone's spindle has frozen,' he said, 'so I came to you.'

'Unload it,' the miller told him. As we loaded and he unloaded, he said something I did not understand and did not even have the courage to inquire about.

'Have you heard the news?' he addressed the miller, in a crass voice. 'The action is coming to take the girls of your village…' The miller hit the mule and handed me the birch branch. 'May you eat it in good health, *inshalla*!'

'Eat what, the oatmeal or this action that is coming to our village to take our girls?' The mule had crossed the wooden river bridge and I had not yet moved from my spot. 'What are you waiting for?' the miller urged me, 'quick, people have no bread…' I wanted to ask him what the action that would come to take our girls was, but I do not know why my mouth had gone dry, my lips were stuck together and I felt like a squalid snowbird.

4

Walking uphill to the village, the mule chose its path through the uphill and I followed. When I caught myself confused and with a mess of a mind, I grabbed the mule by the tail to pull me in its path. The action is coming to take the girls, I mulled. What could this action be? I had never heard that word before. Could it be some man that wants to marry them? Could it be a wild storm just for our girls? Or is it a disease like lice typhoid fever, which will only affect them and not spread to other villages? The mule walked slowly up the steep slope and I could hardly wait to get to the village and ask about this action our girls would be taken by. But who would I ask? Teacher? I had finished the first four grades and it had been almost two years since I started to go around roaming, sometimes with the sheep, sometimes with the goats and, at others, with the donkey; sometimes for water and sometimes for wood; sometimes for blush and sometimes for woodflakes[1], waiting for the seven-grade school to be opened in our village too. '*But this action reached us before the school did,*' I thought. And only for the girls. Not to mention that I did not want to cause trouble to Teacher, whom I had asked so many times about words that I had never heard at home or on the street and I had always disturbed his solitary life.

Initially, I did not know what the word "organisation" meant. It seemed to me like it had something to do with a basement, where some people shouted as to not be heard by others. Then, I was told that it was a place where those who were called "communists" gathered, but no one knew what they did there, even though they shouted: 'This is what the organisation said,' 'this is what the organisation decided,' 'the organisation can cut off your food supply,' 'the organisation can even marry you off if it pleases…'

I once asked someone what drudgery is, but no one explained it to me. Instead, they said, 'You will learn when it falls on your shoulders.' But the worst came to be when I asked what communism is. And I asked the man who had the highest ranks in the army, for whom they had made up a song which was sung only at weddings and only when nobody from the organisation was around…

O Kurtish, kapter i motrës
Pse po shkon si urthi tokës?
Kjo partia, he lum dada
Edhe mutit i dha grada![5]

Then, one day, it reached the ears of some who were not members of the organisation, but who reported to it. Less than a month later, the father of the girl who sang the song was declared *kulak*[6]. On the very same day, they declared *kulak* another man too: someone from the Lower Neighbourhood. He was summoned to the organisation and questioned as to where he had dumped the chemical fertiliser the state had brought from the Soviet Union. 'I threw it in the bushes. It does not do for our land.'

'And you pissed on it,' said another member of the organisation. 'I needed to pee and relieved myself in the bushes.'

'You pissed on Stalin,' the only red-haired man in our village barked in a hoarse voice. 'As long as you pissed on the compost that Father Stalin sent us, it means that you also pissed on him,' the redhead claimed. 'And who says that?'

'I say it!'

'And who do you happen to be, measuring the earth and the sun by your scale?'

'Don't you know? Do you still not know?' threatened the other. 'I lead the organisation and I am the Stalin of this village…' From that day on, both of their names were forgotten: one was labelled the *kulak* who pissed on Stalin, while the other was called "the Stalin of the village", to later be shortened to Salko.

And when I asked Sergeant Kurtish what communism was, it never occurred to me that I would be summoned to the organisation, young as I was. He was puzzled for a moment, masticated a bit, as if to say that he could not find the words to explain it, then grabbed my shirt and said: 'Do you see this shirt? You have one and I don't, we cut it in half and we come out even. Or your mother has

---

[5] O Kurtish, o sergeant of your sister/ Why pass like blight on earth/ This party, bliss on her /Gave ranks even to shit

[6] A term used to label paesants who owned land and were reluctant to support the communist system

a cardigan that she wears in winter and keeps her warm…but my mother does not, we split it in two and give half to my mother. Equality! Communism does not allow your mother to have a cardigan while my mother doesn't. Got it?'

'Got it' I said, 'but this way both of us will be naked, because you can't wear half a shirt and half a cardigan.'

'Where do you get this crooked behaviour from? That Teacher from Shkodra, who was brought here to get into peoples' heads?'

He had been on their bad side since he came to the defence of the one who pissed on Stalin's fertiliser. 'Don't get on his case, he meant no harm,' he had said. But my communism brought him more trouble…I never found out whether it had been Sergeant Kurtish or someone else who had ratted him out to the organisation, but he was summoned to its basement. That was the day I found out why people sounded confused or even scared when they said the words: 'I was summoned by the organisation,' 'it was decided by the organisation,' 'the organisation will distribute grain,' 'he was condemned by the organisation…' In fact, it was not me to be summoned, it was my father. He came back as a storm of dust and stones, grabbed me by my arms and threw me down the stairs. Before I could even get up, he grappled me as if with a hook and bombarded me with slaps and kicks. He pushed, slammed, and tossed me down the basement that was previously owned by one of the escapees, but, later, was taken by the organisation. Along the way, I would occasionally hear people ask about what was happening, as well as the replies: 'Hamza is taking his son to the organisation!' Somewhere near Shelgu i Vjetër[7], Hebil Çobani called out to my father, raising his spotted cane: 'What are you doing, you dishonourable man, you can't just beat the boy up in the streets of the village!'

'When you are the one who gets summoned by the organisation, we'll see what you do,' Father replied. And with these words, I got slapped again and tasted salty blood flowing into my mouth from my nose. At that moment, Majka stepped forward, raised her hands to the sky and hollered: 'Shtoje ovaja nebidnica, more Hamzo, a se pokërvavuje vake sabijence sajbijino? Stram! Stram! Stram!'[8]

Upon these words, my father ceased and he didn't raise his hand on me until we reached the basement door. He shoved me inside, and I could make out

---

[7] The Old Willow

[8] 'What is this ungodliness, o Hamza, is this how you make the sprout of God bleed? Shame, shame, shame!'

21

Salko's red locks, yet I could not recognise the others, even though they were all from my village. I don't know, either from the darkness of the basement or from the ringing in my ears (in those moments I also thought I had gone blind), I was so terrified that my knee cups collided with one another like millstones. Surely, I would have urinated myself had Teacher not entered then.

'What are you doing? Leave the boy alone!'

'You have gotten into his head!' Father said.

'Who taught him these mischievous questions?' Salko asked. 'I did.'

'It is you who should be tried…'

'Do it, but let the boy go…' I somehow started to shiver less, when Anatolia, the old Turkish woman who told me the Scheherazade tales, entered the basement with a shirt and a pair of scissors in her hands.

'What are you doing here?' Salko asked her.

'I came to tell you one thing that you happen to not know.'

'Any of the tales of those one hundred and one nights of yours?' Salko scoffed.

'You dare not pare my nights! They are one thousand and one. Tail off what you are used to, not the nights of my tales,' retorted Anatolia.

She came closer and told me to hold the shirt tightly by one side. She pulled it hard from the other side and cut it into two. Then, she gave one of them to Salko.

'Com'on, put it on and show us all how you'd look. Like a scarecrow, that's how you'd look. Like the devil stuck on a pole scaring us all, that's how you'd look. You and that equality of yours! Let go of the boy, may the sun put its curse on you!'

She went away, throwing Salko the other half of the shirt.

I was also kicked out and nobody ever told me what happened in that organisation after I left. I only know that from then on, they started to leer at him and I tried to ask him as little questions as possible.

However, besides Teacher, I had no one left to ask about that action that was coming. I could not ask my older brother, because after the whole communism affair, he threatened me, wagging his finger: 'Hush you scoundrel, because of you and those questions of yours, they don't accept me into the organisation.' Actually, I was glad, because I didn't want my brother to enter that dim basement.

5

With all these roaming in my head, I hadn't noticed that I was entering the village along with the twilight, just as I was, caught behind the tail of the mule and behind the tails of those words, the meanings of which I didn't know. And I wondered how long the tail of this new word could be, seeing how it would be coming to our village only to take our girls to who-knows-where.

The girls had come out to the gate of the first neighbourhood to sing. They would do so every night. I had asked my grandmother if she had also gone out to sing when she was a girl; we all have sung like that, she responded: me, my mother, grandmother and great-grandmother. The girls would go perch on seven different gates in the village, three in the lower neighbourhood, three in the upper one, and one in that of the Çekors, the smallest one that separated and joined the two larger neighbourhoods. Ever since typhus struck the neighbourhood of Çekors, the girls did not go out to sing there and people did not pass through, but took the path above or below instead, for the fear of typhus. But I had forgotten this fear and was very surprised when I heard the first song that caught my ear:

Haj, more Kurto budalla
Sllushaj shto veli Zejnepa
Ot oves leboj jademe
I pesne ne mise pujet.
Hej, you Kurt, you fool,
Keep listening to what Zejnepa is saying…
Now we are eating oat bread
And the song is stuck in our throats.

I turned red up to the tips of my nails. How did they find out that I had been to the mill to grind oats for bread? And now they are singing my song when I have yet to even enter the village? Who told them, unless it was some bird that

23

flew here from the mill? I looked at them in anger and thought of how glad I was that the action was coming to kidnap them, to quench their bleats and stop them from pointing fingers at us who were forced to eat bread made of oat and the corn of Mursel from Orgosta. When I passed and could no longer hear the song, I thought that we were probably not the first in the village to eat oat. At the second gate, another song was heard.

Haj more Kurto budalla
Sllushaj shto veli Zejnepa…
Enver vo Kukës qe dojde
I zhito qe ni donese…
Hej, you Kurt, you fool
Lend an ear to what Zejnepa is saying…
Enver will come to Kukës
And even bring us grain…

I wondered if this was an old song, from the time Enver Hoxha first came to Kukës four years ago, or if it was a new song and he would come again to bring grain, just as our girls' song went. They sang in front of Murat's gate; it bore this name even though Murat had died many years ago in exile, in Mostar of Bosnia. It was the most famous gate in the village, because it was the only one to still have four bullet holes on it…30 or 40 years ago, the girls had sung just like today, when some unknown men passed through the villages of the Gorge. One of them approached the girls, yet they kept singing. The unknown man touched only one of the singing girls on the shoulder. They screamed and dispersed like frightened quails, beating their wings in a hurry. 'Don't be afraid,' he shouted, 'I am interested in the one I touched. Go and tell people at home that I have betrothed you and you cannot marry anyone but me. I will find you even if you hide like a nut in its shell!' Two weeks later they came again, but, this time, at night. They dug a hole under the room where the girl slept and kidnapped her half-naked. She howled like a bear and woke the whole village up. Someone fired at the kidnappers and they responded to fire with fire. Many bullets were shot, but four of them pierced Murat's gate. The kidnappers escaped, leaving the horror behind and later another song, which the girls sang when they came out at the Gate, a few days later:

Qysh ia lidhën Fatime Dorisë
Duart edhe sytë,
Qysh e futën Fatime Dorinë
Në një thes së dhirtë...[9]

It was later learned that, when the kidnappers came between Nimca and Lojme, they quarrelled over the girl in the sack. 'I will take her,' one said. 'No, I will take her,' said the other. The eldest of them broke some twigs, gathered them in his hand and said: 'choose, the one who picks the short one takes her as his wife.' The shortest twig was picked by the tallest man among the kidnappers and he married the kidnapped girl.

'*But the action will take them all away from us,*' I thought, as I approached the Upper Neighbourhood, '*my sister too?*' I frightened myself.

---

[9] How did they tie Fatime Dori's/ Hands and eyes,/ How did they throw Fatime Dori/Into a goat wool sack.

6

As I approached the Burnt Mosque, the girls' song was replaced by Craple's—
the village teller's—cries. 'Hear ye, hear ye!' I started shaking…

I was afraid of this man and could not say why. Whether it was due to his
bear-like walk or his hoarse voice, with which he gave the news and made calls
and announcements for the village. Perhaps I was most frightened by his left
hand, on which the thumb was missing. Some said that he had cut it while hewing
beams for his house; others said that he had worked on the construction of the
railway from Durrës to Peqin; a handful of insidious red-wasp-like words were
also thrown here and there by some wicked women in the village, or even some
troublemaking men, who said that he was caught stealing cattle in Tetovo, and
the shepherds cut off his thumb with shears. But in the village, he was known as
an honest man. His hand-stump was heavy. While working as the guard of the
village canal, he once caught me taking water out of turn to a small field, where
we planted squash as well as pinto and white kidney beans. In fact, I had not
been taking the water to irrigate, but for a contraption which scared away the
badger that ate our corn. Father had tied our dog to scare the corn-eaters away
with his barks, and I would bring him food every day; I wanted to cry when I
had to leave and his groans sounded like a baby's wails. With my uncle's eldest
son, who was handy, we came up with a rattling contraption that spun with water
and hit a metal sheet, frightening the animals that would eat our corn. But right
on the second day, when I wanted to add more water, Craple jumped in front of
me as if he had sprouted from the ground, or fallen from a clear blue sky.

'Are you stealing water, Hamza's little chicklet?'

'I do not steal, but…' I replied, unable to take my eyes off his stump.
Breathless still, my ear rang from the blow, the world began spinning and I fell,
breaking a corn branch that did not manage to hold my weight. He pulled back,
but that bear-like image was ingrained in my mind, even though I had heard good
words about him being a man who lived on his own bread and rags. His hand-

stump appeared in front of my eyes even in that moment, when he was clearing his throat and I anticipated that he was going to give some ghastly news. 'Hear ye, hear ye...!'

We had had two criers, one for the Upper Neighbourhood and another for the Lower one. This had always been the case until the day Stalin died, three or four years ago. They were both summoned by the organisation to be given instructions on how to announce the news, Craple went immediately, but the other crier, Çinarçe (I do not know why they called him that), had disappeared. He was not at home, not at the big trunk where the men of the Upper Neighbourhood would congregate, they searched the garden since his wife said that he had gone to kill the mole that would eat their cabbages, but they did not find him there either. Then Craple spread the word throughout the village, shouting: 'Great grief in Albania, Father Stalin died in Russia!' It was later learned that Çinarçe, a short but strong-voiced man, had been hiding in the haystack until he heard the other crier shout: 'Great grief in Albania, Father Stalin died in Russia.' From that day on, they both, Craple and Çinarçe, no longer divided the work of the crier based on the neighbourhoods, but according to the message that would be given: bad news was taken over by Craple, good ones by Çinarçe.

I was recalling this when I heard Craple shouting, 'Hey, peasants. Hear ye, hear ye! Today, as soon as the sun sets, the village will gather—one person from each house—in the yard of the Council, at Shahin's Café! There is a conference! There is a conference for the girls who will go to the plant action. Hey, hear ye, hear ye!'

Conference...girls...conferact...hear ye, hear—ye...I could not even understand how the words were mingling with each other, as if they were pushing, spitting and grabbing each other by the hair... Conference...girlact...girlplant...my sister...

I had reached the small square in front of the fountain. The bear was still there, no one paid her any mind. To me, it seemed as if another bear, lively and stately, was throwing its paws over the village. Only the water of the fountain kept flowing with the same rustling as it had flowed hundreds of years ago when three women found it there and wet their parched lips.

27

7

No one knew when and by whom the first house of my village had been built, not even those of the province of Gora, of which it was a part. All that was known was that at one point, the first people of the village had settled somewhere below, on the river bank, in a place called Gushaja, where almost all the inhabitants contracted a bothersome disease that made their goitres swell and look like bags of oat, especially those of women. The women had been the first to decide to uproot themselves from that place, one of them even made an eight-hour walk to Tetovo and another just as long to Prizren, just to have the most famous gownsmen of those areas prepare *bazibén* and talismans.

Some prepared them talismans and took the money, one of them did not take the gold he was owed, but tried to bed the woman, meanwhile one of the gownsmen, who was much like a half-doctor, kindly told her that they would not benefit from prayers or talismans, as long as they didn't change the water they drank. 'You must find your *abuzamzam*, your holy water of the Ka'bah,' he told her. Then she took two other women along and one early morning they went uphill towards the Black Peak and looked for water. They searched across the beeches, meadows, junipers and wherever else they set foot. Just like those Arab soldiers who were looking for water in Spain and when they found it, they shouted 'Mahadrid, some water' and settled in the place that is now called Madrid. The three women of Gushaja did not call out, but instead filled some vases from those springs that seemed to have lighter water. They did so for many more days, until they felt more at ease with the irritability caused by their drooping goitres, which even seemed to have become smaller.

From that day forth, they started to move from Gushaja to this new settlement, which they named Bukojna, because it had a beech forest with numerous water springs, the best of which was the one they named Topillo, which many, many years later became the centre of the village, on which Sinan Pasha of Kallabak built a mosque and right in front of its burnt ruins, the border soldiers would put the scaffold to show the villagers the slain bear and of which Salko had said: 'Why did you have to cross the border, it was pretty comfortable in the forest.' When the three women went up in search of water, for the first time in their lives, they saw the mountains and hills surrounding the village and the province, and which, from that pit by the river where their houses were, could not be seen.

'There is an entirely different world out here,' said one of them.

'Let's settle here, at least we can look at this world,' said the other.

'And look how many stones there are,' said the third. Then, they were reminded of the legend that was told about Gora and Goran from the time when their grandparents had not yet been born. It was said that when the news that God would assemble all the provinces to share the goods he owned came, Goran set out and travelled for nine days and nine nights without stopping, until he reached the House of God. But when he arrived, the table had already been cleared.

'Where do you come from?' God asked.

'From the end of the world,' he answered.

'You are late. I shared all the goods I had.'

'Lord, I travelled for nine days and nine nights to reach your garden. Don't send me back empty-handed.' God looked around the garden, took a stone and gave it to him. 'I have this and I give it with all my heart, maybe you will have few things in life, but you will love the stones of your mountains profoundly.'

'Eh', sighed one of the three women, 'he did not give us anything else to love…' And she remembered that the people of the village opposite from theirs expressed love for their land rather strangely:

'Borje oboreno, Sërce izgoreno.'[10]

'Their hearts burn with longing even for the cliffs and chutes,' she said out loud.

* * *

I had gathered all these from fragments of conversations, one here and one there, and one day I told them to Teacher, who held an hour-long lesson asking us what we knew about our province. Many days later, on a Holy Night and on which my mother had made *fli*[11], she set a plate aside, wrapped it in white cloth

---

[10] For wrecked Borje, burns the heart

[11] A pastry dish, considered a traditional specialty of the region

and gave it to me to take it to Teacher. Let him also eat a little bit of *fli*. Who knows how long it has been since he has had a bite from his mother's hand. Teacher lived in one room of a house, the owner of which had fled to the other state a few years ago. The other rooms of the house were occupied by the postman and a woman, whom some said was his sister and others believed to be his wife.

When I took the *fli* to Teacher, he told me to sit on the only chair in the room. He tasted it, liked it a lot and asked what it was. 'Fli[12],' I said. 'What do you mean? It's still early.' Then I explained to him that what he was eating was called *fli* but had nothing to do with sleep. As he enjoyed his meal, I looked around the room, where, in addition to the books we studied in class, on a small shelf, there were other books, as well. I had only seen the school books and my father's Koran which was recited it in the mosque for Eid. 'Who makes these books?' I asked.

'Writers, poets. Here, look. This is Naim Frashëri, this is Mjeda, and this other, Gjergj Fishta. I talked to you about Naim at school, don't you remember? The other two are from my hometown. I got to know them, one from afar and the other more intimately; we were from the same neighbourhood in Shkodra. 'I wanted to ask him how those who make books can be the same as us, since Prophet Muhammad was not the same as us. But it seemed difficult for me to get involved in these thickets which I did not know how to enter or leave. However, I was amazed that there were books written on earth and not just what God had dictated to Muhammad from heaven. I really liked the stories of those books I listened to in the mosque after the Eid prayers. Especially that story of the saint who came down from heaven with a white ram and told the man on earth, do not sacrifice your son, sacrifice the ram that I brought you.

I related this to Teacher. He smiled and then took another book and showed it to me. Three thousand years before Muhammad was born, the great Homer wrote about these. Browsing and showing me excerpts from the book, Teacher seemed like he had left his room and was instead flying around the house. I wanted to fly too, but I could not move because someone had tied me to the chair with some invisible rope. Then his voice ceased, and I noticed that he was there again, sitting on the corner of the bed, lost in a mist mixed with rays of light penetrating here and there from his eyes and below his eyes.

---

[12] "Fli" in Albanian is also the imperative form of verb fle—sleep

'We have our own Homer as well,' he said, 'but the whereabouts of his remains are unknown, they have wiped his grave out.'

I trembled with fear, just as I had on the day our village was stuck by a great downpour that lasted for several days and in the streets of the village I heard men and women shouting: 'Move! Quickly! Deluge has struck the graveyard, and the dead have risen and are going down into the river.'

I came to learn later that the storm had uprooted and destroyed the graves along the creek and mingled the remains of the dead. The villagers had tried to collect them from the creek and put them back in some new graves, further away from the creek. They narrated that Nefka and Ollman had been about to fight over an arm bone because they both thought it belonged to their grandfathers. 'It is bad when the living quarrel over the affairs of the dead,' Majka said, and the bone affair was settled, I don't know how. Such a deluge must have reached Teacher's city too, but I didn't ask him any further, for I was afraid of the answer I would hear. But it was him to ask me, and he asked me to tell him once again the history of the village and the legend of the province, as I had heard it from others. When I was done, he took another book from the shelf and said to me:

'When you grow up, you will probably study these things, but I want to tell you what others have written about you, the Gorani people…'

'Eight hundred years ago, a heresy that did not obey the dogmas of the Church of the time was born in the Balkans. The heretics denied the sin of our origins and clarified the affairs of the world in their own way, proclaiming the existence of two gods, two creators, two principles for all things. 'How can a God who has done so much good also cause so much evil in this world?' they would ask. Therefore, according to them, there were two, the God of good and the God of evil. The first had created the invisible and spiritual things, the second the visible and material things; good deeds were the work of the first whereas the evil ones in the second. This heresy devastated many countries and peoples, even our Illyria for several years. Mani, the founder of this heresy, was flayed alive by the order of the king of Persia, while Emperor Diocletian had the leaders of this religion burnt alive. So did Robert, the King of France. In Constantinople, Emperor Alexius Comnenus had monk Basil, the leader of the heretical Bogomils, burned at the stake. These heretics in Bulgaria were called Bogomils, the benefactors of God; in Asia they were called Palicians, in France Albigeois and in Italy by the name Albanians…And here, in these parts, they are called

31

bagholders, driven away and wandering all their lives with a bag in their hands…'

As he was explaining these things, Teacher suddenly closed the book, looked at me in astonishment, and said: 'Did you know these? Have you heard of them before?'

'No', I said, 'I hadn't, but Majka had once told me of a grandfather or great-grandfather of hers who had been captured by the king of the Bulgarians. He had his people burned in a fire; others killed in torture, and more others sent to roam the world barefoot and with no food. As for Majka's great-grandfather, he had his tongue cut off, so that he could no longer speak, because the king was afraid of his words. Thus spoke Majka. And so, tongue-less, he roamed the mountains and hills, until he came and settled in these mountains of ours.'

'And who is this Majka?' Teacher asked.

'Ah, you don't know her? She is an old woman who has lived two or three hundred years on this earth and of whom death has forgotten about. Her house is nearby. She can heal one with magic. She has healed me too…'

I immediately regretted telling him this, but it was too late. Teacher became very curious about my illness and the magic of Majka who had healed me. Hence, I had to tell him that following the day that my father was summoned to the basement of the organisation because of me, as I had said that communism leaves people naked, that they want to split a shirt it into two or three to make people equal, and when my father slapped and kicked me and handed me over to the organisation, only Majka had stepped forth on the street and called out to him: 'What is the matter with you? How can you beat the sprout of God in the middle of the road? May the devil cross your path!' and she had tried to hit him with her century-old cane, but the father had dodged, saying that not only the devil in person but also the devil's mother already had. And so, exactly after that day, I was afflicted with a disease between my thighs and under my belly and something that resembled the white lung of a cow appeared on both of my legs. My mother took me to Majka and she said: 'This struck the boy from the distress of the basement!'

From the shelf, she took a basket made of thin willow branches, and from there, she took two carved wooden spoons, a rake with strings, and began to burn the strings and strike the spoons, and gently blew air towards the spot where the two cow lung marks had appeared. They are my great grandfather's spoons, she told me when I asked, the one whose tongue was cut off so as to not let him

32

speak. I went to Majka for three days in a row, but the cow lungs would not disappear from my thighs. We will go to church, she told me on the third day. My mother was bewildered: Where did this church come from? We only knew of a church in your Shkodra and that the church kills and burns people. No, no, Majka told me, there is a church here in our village. I knew that lower down, near the river, in Ograd, there was a black stone called Fshati i Priftit[13], but I had never been there.

Majka got on our mule and, as I held it by the bridle, we went down to the Priest's Village. She had brought the spoons and strings with her, but she had also taken three candles. When she lit them, she spoke in a low voice, as if she was speaking to herself, but I managed to hear her words. I am lighting the first for you, O Lord, and hear my words…I am lighting the second for you, O ancestor and follower of God, and hear my words…I am lighting the third for you, O man who was burned for the church and who took shelter here…In a blackened niche I noticed countless remnants of burnt candles and I asked Majka about the priest who had been burned. They did not burn him, she told me, but hung him upside down from the big oak tree in Bërce and lit a pile of rye straw below. They threw straw at him and his hair would have caught on fire had he not surrendered. Fine, he said at last, I'm giving you the keys to the church. But the next day, he left the village and came here to Ograd, where he set up his own village, on this big stone and where no one came to visit him until he died that very same winter.

Later on, people started coming here to light candles and many have been healed by his soul. After saying a few more prayers, Majka entered a garden planted with cabbage, plucked two large leaves, and wrapped them around my thin thighs, where the cow's lungs had appeared. 'These will heal you,' she told me. 'These, or your magic?'

'All together, son, all: the cabbage, and God, and milk, and magic, and honey, and the priest.' She did not mention the hodja and I knew the reason. She had a sister in the village and, when she died, she had left nothing to be given to the imam for the funeral services, and he asked the village to cover those expenses, but when the village also had nothing to offer him, the imam cut two plum roots from the garden of the dead woman and said, 'Well, I'm taking the compensation myself.' I was well-versed in all of Majka's stories and Teacher stared at me with curiosity.

---

[13] The Priest's Village

'Shall we go to Majka?'

His question came to me so suddenly that I responded with another question: 'Are you sick?' He told me he wanted to meet this three-hundred-year-old woman, as I had told him, and we got up.

8

The door was opened to us by one of her nephews or great-grandchildren, telling us that Majka was busy. 'With whom?' I asked. 'With Salko,' he told me. He has been bitten by a snake and Majka is performing magic on him. Truthfully, she had the two wooden spoons in her hands to which she had even added an iron rod, and, in a basket nearby, there were some chickens that were clucking like crazy; they were all black. Majka would take them one by one, slash their behinds, and place them on the serpent's wound. Salko groaned...'I am gonna die, I'm gonna die. Please Majka, don't let me die.' 'No, Majka will not let that happen. The basement would be deserted without you,' would she answer. The chickens died, one after the other, absorbing the snake venom with their bottoms. One of the brides of the house would put the dead ones in an old sack and take the living ones out of the basket and hand them to Majka, so she could place their asses on Salko's foot. Finally, one of the chickens stood up, as if numb, but her legs held her and she walked through the yard. 'They took all the poison out,' Majka claimed.

'Did I make it?' asked a petrified Salko.

'A little more, a little more,' said the time-worn woman. 'What's started by the chicken's ass will be finished by the dog's ass.' She took a pot from the stove and gave it to him. 'You will drink this tea I made with herbs and a piece of dog shit and you will become fit as a fiddle.'

'Oh I'd not only drink dog shit, but also pork shit!' he exclaimed. 'We only have dogs here...' Majka said.

When she was finished and saw him out, she turned to us as if to ask: what have you been bitten by? I told her that Teacher's wanted to meet her, but she was paying no attention to my words and called out to the young bride.

'Prepare some coffee for the Teacher,' she said in a low but very commanding voice. 'The Teacher seems to want some stories,' she said, speaking to herself rather than to us who may just as well not have been there.

'Stories…Is that right, Teacher?' Teacher nodded and in his eyes I noticed desire and curiosity. 'Well, Teacher who came from Shkodra to teach our children, know that in this world there is only one story…of what man was, what he is and what he will be. Nothing has been, is or will last forever, what may have been one beautiful day, will cease to be on the next…And as for our village, you could speak or write, as I have learned that you write…Write, then, that somewhere at the end of the world or nowhere at all, hidden in the fog, is a village called Bukojna, the men of which turn grey when still children and see better at night than at daylight. Do you know, Teacher, what they say about the men and boys of our village? They were not born out of their mothers' wombs but out of the fog of Kallabak. From the moment they are born and until they die, they are the children of fog. They wrap them in diapers of fog when they come out of the mother's womb and put them in shrouds of fog when they are escorted behind the Kodra[14], to the cemetery. And all their life passes as fog around the world, they snatch the autumn winds wherever they can, embrace the rocks in river beds, share bread with the night and quarrel with the day…We worry about this world and the next world a lot…I had a dog that ate my chickens here in the yard. One, two, three…When your own dog eats your chickens, it is like being robbed by a member of the household. I thought to myself, '*better without a dog than without chickens*,' and I threw my herbs to its lap, and the next day the boys took it and buried it away. I didn't even ask them where. But now, O Teacher, I am terrified. I called Çinarçe and gave him a gold coin, which had been placed on my forehead when I entered this house as a bride. Take it, I told him and dig a grave twice as deep for me. And do you know why, Teacher? I dream every night as if dogs hollow out my grave and pull my bones out…'

The bride brought coffee. Majka ordered her to place it on the window sill.

'No, no, I have it hot,' said Teacher, thinking that they were placing the cup on the ledge for the coffee to cool.

'Drink it as you please, but wait until it gets into your hands…I heard that you teach these crumb-crunchers that the world revolves, right?'

'Yes, yes,' said Teacher, as if caught up in guilt.

'Well, wait for the world to revolve, as you say, sir, and the coffee will come into your hands by itself …'

My chest was almost bursting from the laughter I was holding in, but I contained myself, because I was sorry and ashamed for Teacher, and I was afraid

---

[14] The Hill

36

of some new magic form Majka. She noticed it and said: 'Go, otherwise your mother will worry. The Teacher and I will talk about the affairs of the two worlds.'

I was about to leave, but with the door half open, I turned to her: 'What sort of snake bit Salko that made you give him tea with dog shit? You heal others only with black chickens…'

'Yes, but how can he heal without dog shit? He is such a scalawag, this redhead of our village. He tricked me once, I will remember it even in the hereafter…He called me in the basement and asked me: what will happen tomorrow?

Do you, sorcerer, know what will happen tomorrow? The moon will block the path of the sun. I almost died upon hearing those words, there in the basement, and all night-long I did not find comfort in bed. But that dog had read it in the newspaper and burned all the newspapers that came to the village, so that no one could learn what was going to happen. He gathered a lot of men and called me too. Come on, sorcerer, save the Sun from the Moon! What was there to see! Suddenly the moon put its fingers in the sun's eyes and blinded it; it became night in the middle of the day! We were all scared, but Stalin called out to us: "Do not be afraid, now I will free the Sun from the Moon!" Before he could even finish his words, daylight came again…You know, it was the *calipse*, or whatever you call it.'

I closed the door and ran away, thinking of stories that Majka and Teacher would tell each other.

9

The men of Gushaja had travelled far, far away to learn about the disease of their village. They asked the wisest men of seven provinces, but each gave a piece of their own mind, not at all resembling what the others had said. They only stopped searching for a cure when a Turkish imam in the small mosque of Prizren told them that everyone could be cured of that disease, once they found and built their houses in a place where the sun rises twice a day and the moon disappears twice a night. We're condemned by God, the men of Gushaja said, and they submitted to this divine punishment. But the women kept searching, and when they reached the foot of the Black Peak, one morning, they noticed that the sun they had just seen had disappeared. They ran further, and, when they crossed a hill, they saw the sun rising again between the two peaks, on the crowns of beeches. Here it is, they called, and did not want to wait until nightfall to check the moon. Just here, between the two mountains, the sun rises twice, and this is where we will build our houses.

For many years to come, all those who left to change their settlement, either due to some disease, poverty, or to escape some blood feud foe, asking here and there, met someone who told them that if you want to be saved, go to the village where the sun rises twice every day and the moon disappears twice every night. As far as twelve generations back and even more recently, other families and households came to Bukojna. Its first inhabitants called them *doshlanë*[15]…After all, they did not have roots there either, but had come hundreds of years ago, when persecuted by crusaders and priests, with swords and scissors in hand to kill them, to cut off their arms, or even worse, to cut off their tongues so that, wherever they went, they would never again say that in heaven and earth, there are two Gods: one, the God of good and the other, the God of evil. Hence, they accepted newcomers to the village even five centuries after their ancestors; they

---

[15] denizen

offered them a hearth, and then visited them. They even married the ones already in this village, which was not the case in the villages beyond Gjallica.

In most cases, the newcomers did not bring trouble; on the contrary, they had escaped trouble…The Shunds came first, after a highlanders' bloody quarrel in their lands, where, for a sheepfold fence, for a puddle, or for a handful of salt for the sheep, they had been killed and slaughtered by seed and tribe. The first from the Shunds came along with eight other people, but the other eight were all female: his wife and seven daughters, while the other males had left their bones in the mountains and cliffs. He also brought with him a ram and a sheep from which he later made the largest herd in the village, the herd that grew up with his seven daughters. The girls grew up to become young ladies, and, then, the people in the village realised they were the most beautiful young girls in the world or the most beautiful that they had set eyes upon. Soon the boys began to sing a song that even today, after hundreds of years, has two of its verses hanging on the cherry blossoms:

'Zajde sënce megju dve pllanine,
A ja legna megju dve vllahine'

When the Teacher who came from Shkodra heard them, he translated them for us, and we memorised and sang them to the girls, many of whom were probably the great-granddaughters of the seven beautiful girls of the first Shund. 'The sun went down between the two mountains, I lay down between two Vlach women!' Today, there is a small neighbourhood within the Lower Neighbourhood called "the Shunds", but surely the seeds of the first Shund have been planted in all the gardens of the two large neighbourhoods: both the lower and the upper.

Then the child of two Jews came. He would disappear into the darkness every passing year and bring to the village all the inventions of the world, from the binoculars my grandmother used to the one the oldest among them called "the box that does not forget", a brown box under whose lid a black plate would rotate after being wound up and, when you stuck a needle in, it would start singing. 'Does it never forget the song?' My grandmother once asked, and the elder of the Isaacs said, 'Never ever, this is the box that remembers.'

At first, it only remembered songs coming from beyond Tetovo: about a bird drinking water on the side of Vardar, or about Biljana washing clothes in its waters, and I did not know if this Vardar was a fountain, a spring or a stream. I later learned that it was a river as long as our Black Drin, with only one difference; they flowed in opposite directions. Then, shortly before the war, when an Italian major came to the village, in addition to soccer balls and T-shirts that had the word "Juve" written on the back, he brought some other black plates and the box began to also remember Italian songs as well as another that was sung to a certain Xhixhile, but it was not to be understood why they sang this song to her. In our parts, when one sings a song to girl, the reason is clear…Once, a girl from Zapodi married the sergeant of our village and they sang to her 'Azize, beautiful girl, yours is such an oddity.' Or the famous song about Xhemula of Krusheva, who after being driven away by her mother-in-law, a wicked tiny crooked woman, she remarried in Shishtavec with a wedding three times bigger than the first. Or that other song for Zarifa from a village in Gryka e Vanave[16] who was kidnapped by a man that forced her to be his wife and they sang to her: 'Oh plump Zarife, why did you not sleep with a gun? What could I, poor Zarife, do, when my drawstring fell into the river…' And the last plate that came for the box-that-did-not-forget was on some murders and generals…'On August 7, forty nine, news reached Tirana, today the entirety of Mirdita is weeping, our comrade Bardhok Biba was murdered, Mehmet Shehu stood up, ordered General Gjini to…,' and I do not know how it went on. I remember all this because the boys of that household were my cousins, as my grandmother had married off one of her daughters to the household of all the inventions of the world. Unless I brought them sweet pears from our garden, they refused to open the magic box for me. One day, when there were no more pears left, I said, 'I know the real name of this box, my brother told me, it is called gramophone.'

"Gramashit", jumped the elder, 'what do you mean?' When I told him that it was recording the voices so that it would not forget, he called out to me: 'Potayto, potahto! That is also what our grandfather is saying: it remembers, it does not forget.'

* * *

The third wave of newcomers was not received with much enthusiasm. Actually, there was a strife that went on for days: whether to accept them or not. Their chief had killed a boy with his own hands and some said that we do not

---

[16] The Gorge of Vanas

want killers in our village, others defended him claiming that he killed for honour, a third group did not interfere and waited for those who quarrelled every evening in a cellar—where the men of the village had coffee—to decide. In time, it was learned where from and why that tall, straight man of white hair and a black pipe and who had arrived with four loaded horses, his children and a woman who was said to be mad, came.

He came from the Cursed Mountains and it was soon learned what had driven him here to the Sharr Mountains. It was said that he was a very reputable man, who owned a saddle horse, watch chain and pistol, but things turned sour when one day, he found his wife at the haystacks with a young boy from the village, clinging to each other like mallows and meowing like cats in February. He had taken his pistol out and pointed it at them, but he had not fired it. He had told the boy to get up and leave and sent him away, saying:

'I'm not killing you, but beware that your mouth might.'

The boy ran away with his stuff in hand and did not even have time to think about the man he had just dishonoured. Many months later, while he was chatting and joking with friends, the man passed by and everyone stood up to honour him, only the one who had been caught with his wife, did not move. 'Why are you standing for him?' he asked. 'The whole highland honours Gjek standing up,' they replied. 'Well, I don't have to move, because he found me with his wife and here, I am alive among you …' The word made its way to Gjek's ear, and he went to the yard of his wife's lover right away:

'Had I warned you, beware that your mouth might kill you?' and had emptied all the bullets of his pistol.

He did not run away from the rifle, but since the day he found her with her lover, his wife neither ate nor drank. 'Kill me,' she would tell her husband, and when he killed the lover, she ran away from home with no headscarf. Gjek's wife went mad, people said. Nobody knew where she went and got lost. One day Gjek went to Ulcinj and in the Bazaar he saw a crazy woman who went from store to store uttering meaningless words. The left side of his face froze, because she looked like his wife who had run away from home with no headscarf. 'Whose are you, o noble woman?' he asked her and received a bullet-like answer. 'I'm the bride of Gjek Gjeloshi.' He asked around the Bazaar and was told that they did not know her, but that she said to anyone who asked her: 'I am the wife of Gjek Gjeloshi.' He looked for her again, found her, mounted her on the saddle horse, and took her home. The evil within is not to be thrown out, he said, and that very day he decided to leave his village.

When the madwoman died, our village did not allow her to be buried in the cemetery. They told him that a little further the giaour[17] cemetery, which dated before Turkey, was to be found, and there, she was buried. Even now, two or three hundred years later, after they have mingled with the village in marriage and kinship, and after they have converted to Islam, their dead are still buried where they had dug the first grave of the family. It is still said that the first son of their tribe, Nik Gjeloshi, who fell in love with a girl from the Shunds, died shortly before his wedding, just the day the wedding commenced. God knows why, his fiancée had told him that she would not marry him unless he got circumcised. He loved the girl and granted her wish, but because the barber of Cërnaleva was some other place, he was circumcised at the barber of Pakisha who was not that skilled. The poor boy got infected and died and, in front of the grave, Gjek Gjeloshi spoke in such a way as if he were convinced that the dead man was listening to him: 'Oh son, with Christ you broke up, with Muhammad you did not meet; only the devil knows where they are going to take you!' Following that death, their neighbourhood took the name of Nik, and they adopted the customs of the village and unified with them in all except for the cemetery that they preserved for generations, that of the giaour.

So many are the descendants of the first three caravans, that most don't know whether they descend from Shunds, the Jews or the Highlanders. Gora is all stones and rocks, as far as seven provinces away, but its heart is as soft as the *revani*[18] dessert they prepare and which sucks the syrup smoothly. But the people of Bukojna themselves said that every caravan that came added something to us: the first added to our beauty, the second to our wisdom, and the third strengthened our hearts. Hence, when people heard that it was a land where the sun rose twice and the moon set twice, they would go after it and, even if they did not settle, they would never forget it.

---

[17] İnfidel, non-muslim

[18] A traditional semolina cake that is often served well-saturated in sugar syrup

10

Yet, the last settler had a harder time with our village. For six years, he was given permission neither for a fireplace nor for grave, although it was not his fault; it was mostly because of the bandits he befriended. He came to the village as a seymen to guard the houses from thieves, who, when the men were afield, stole whatever they found: cattle, bedding and garments, horses and donkeys, even the bread in the dough bowl. It was said that, years ago, one of our villagers had been killed just to rob the three pairs of *opingas*[19] he had bought in Prizren and was bringing home. They had lurked in Buka, behind a bush, and flattened him. The bandits had blocked the way of another and he had resisted, at first, but when they raised their rifles, he handed them the horse, telling them in a broken Albanian: 'I have other hose...you kill for *opinga,* let alone for a saddle hose...'

Because of the deeds of his fellow craftsmen, the new protector was not much venerated, as for bravery they likened him to nobody. In 1918, the province of Gora was placed under the administration of the Serbs, as the border would move back and forth whenever the evil winds of politics blew. The bandits operating at the time were thirty-six. They had been declared "wanted" and at the top of the list was also the bandit of Kolloshtreza, because he had murdered the secretary of the Prefecture of Prizren, who was found naked and with no boots, thrown in a field. It was learned that the Serb had been killed by the Kolloshtreza bandit from a telegram he himself sent to Bajram Curri.

This is how the bandits lived their lives, sometimes fighting for themselves, sometimes for their homeland, and quite often the dividing line between theft and politics was not clear. A thin thread separates good from evil among them, said Mullah Isuf of Bukojna, the man who had more books in his home than all those of the others put together. Because he was the most knowledgeable of all, he tried hard to convince the International Boundary Commission to include

---

[19] Traditional rubber or leather shoes, somehow similar to moccasins

Gora as a whole within the territory of Albania, but he managed to have only a quarter of it placed there. He had books, but not the golden coins of Serbia, which along Prizren took 18 of the villages of Gora. When Zog became king and they no longer fought for borders, the Kolloshtreza bandit came to our village and asked to live there. They did not give him permission! Yet he was not dejected by their refusal and started to build a water canal, to irrigate the fields and gardens in Ograda. The water only brought him closer to the village. 'If waters mix, blood boils,' Majka had warned. 'It is said in vain that people kill for blood. In fact, people kill for water!'

When he was given the right to smoke/permission, he built a house with a well in the yard, because he did not want to send the women of the house to the village fountain for water. Occasionally his comrades raided the village and he was the one who was held responsible. 'Why do you keep coming here,' he would tell them, and one day, to get rid of them all, he told them to follow him as he would show them where they could plunder and not disturb this poor village of refugees. And they went to steal the dowry of a rich girl in Tetovo, but it was their last robbery. Someone from the girl's house fired a pistol and the bullet hit the Kolloshtreza bandit. Either the bullet was poisoned, or because he walked for two days in snow and mud, his leg got gangrenous, and he died within three weeks. The whole village and plenty of bandits from the villages across Gjallica attended his funeral. At the time, but even today, in our village, before burying the dead, the imam asks: 'Hey congregation, do you bestow *halal*[20] to the dead? Bestowed…Once, twice, three times.' This is also what the imam asked for the bandit of Kolloshtreza. Most said halal, halal, but whispers were also to be heard. 'How did you know this man, o congregation?' The imam asked again.

'Allahbiler,' said one. 'God knows!'

'Kimbiler,' said another. 'Who knows!'

'Hajnbiler', said the third, and this was Mullah Isuf. 'Thieves know!' The bandits perked up and one of them took out his pistol and put it on his forehead, just below the turban. Mullah Isuf took out his. Very few people knew that, besides the turban and the books, he had brought from Prizren a silver pistol crafted by one of the gun makers of the ancient city, which Mulla Isuf did not call by its name, but referred to as "The City of Heaven". The mouths of the two revolvers looked at each other and the eyes of the two men flashed facing one

---

[20] In Islamic tradition, the bestowal of halal for the dead implies forgiving their wrongdoings and forsaking their debts

another. 'I saw myself in his eyes,' Mullah Isuf would later remark. But the leader of the bandits called out to his friend: 'Put down your weapon, you can't shoot a turban!' The very same day the bandit was buried, they went to Tetovo and looted and burned down the house from which their friend was shot.

The family of the bandit did not leave our village and, to this day, it has the most beautiful gate, with a Prizren plank and large Mostar plinths, just like on the gates of palaces. Even though the most beautiful gate and even though some of its boys married village girls, nobody ever gathered to sing in front of that house.

'Do not tread where theft and pulitics mix,' Majka would say.

'It is called politics and not pulitics,' Salko would correct her upon hearing it.

'Call it cocktics if you like, it's the same,' she would reply. 'All those who have come and settled in our village, have escaped trouble and did not bring trouble, until what you call politics and I called pulitics arrived. Since then, the table does not feed, the pillow does not comfort and the spring does not refresh. And you know why? Because its twin sister is theft. We will hear his cry one day and our brains will whirl as if in a storm, and it will rush to change our blood and soul.'

11

Three days after the first conference, no family had yet agreed to send their girls to the action. We did not give birth to daughters to give them to the action, their mothers would say. They said these words at home, while sweeping the yard, when fetching water from the fountain or when they took the cattle there to drink, when they made the bread in the bowl, and they kept talking to themselves even when they laid the dough on the pan. On the other hand, the men kept silent. They talked to themselves, but not to each other. They feared that their word might grow feet and go down to the basement, where Salko, at one of the conferences, had said that if he had a hundred sisters, he would have sent them all to action. Then, as if by accident and allegedly unintentionally, he had reminded them of the murdered bear. She had stepped on the soft belt, and thus the entire load of an automatic gun had been emptied on her, he said. The soft belt was a wide strip of land, finely worked; it stretched along the length of the border, which separated us from the other state. And our village had a very long border line, almost a full circle, with only one exit: in the direction of Gryka e Vanave. All the fields and meadows beyond the soft belt were barren and not mowed. Hundreds of other acres of fields, meadows, forests had been taken from us years ago, when some people with the strange name of Border Defining Commission came from Russia, France or England. Once, when Father and I went to work the land on that side, waving his hand, he told me that our lands were over there. Beyond. 'The whole meadow under cobblestones is ours; there are more than eight acres, at the top there is also a very good water spring, clear water.' We looked at them from a distance, and we could neither go back to work the land, nor to graze the sheep, to gather grass or wood, or to look for strawberries. Soldiers guarded on both sides of the border and it was terrifying to step on the soft belt and if you dared to cross over, you'd be bullet-ridden like the bear! Only after the bear was killed did I feel the real horror of an adventure that happened to me two years ago. While grazing the cows by the soft belt, I glanced in the direction of our meadow and noticed a magnificent flower patch; I had never laid my eyes on more beautiful flowers. Our soldiers had moved down, towards Guri i Shqipes[21] and I was sure that I could escape their eyes, but I did not know where the ones of the other state could have hid. Even now I do not grasp the craze that overcame me, and I turned into a rabbit to reach our meadow, which was no longer ours, since when the two states quarrelled and grow bitter with each other, eight years ago. I quickly picked up the first flowers that came to hand and ran away. I expected them to call me from behind 'Stoj, ne merdaj!', but there was just a murderous silence. When I passed over the soft belt, it seemed to me that I had left my heart and lungs across the border; I could not breathe and I realised I was in a state of shock from the fear. I took the flowers home and lied, saying I had picked them up in the forest. I never did tell anyone about my foolishness for that bouquet. If the soldiers had seen me, Salko would have said that he stepped on the soft belt to get meadow flowers, so he took the bullet.

Stepped on the soft belt…do not step the belt…stepping kills…bear flowers or meadow flowers…I thought these while I walked like a sleepwalker in the village streets. I went to the seven gates, where the girls gathered. They were singing, as if there was no action in the world, as if there was no Craple that interrupted their song every evening, calling 'tonight there is a conference, a person from every household should attend;' as if there was no basement, where some red-haired Stalin in rubber shoes pointed his finger to the soft belt with a strange ferocity those days, as if the guards had killed the bear just to scare the peasants. They kept singing, and I wondered if they would be able to sing in the action, where the girls of my village would be taken. From the very first day I heard that peasant at the mill saying that the action would come to take the girls to our village, I imagined the action to be as I saw it in the dream the first night: like a black hole with burnt thorns that swallowed the girls one by one. It would take them away from the song and put them in its huge mouth. At times, it seemed to me that someone caught them and threw them in the mouth of a wild animal, a mouth as big as a basement door, but I would wake up even more scared when I saw the girls being thrown naked into a well, only a kerchief on their heads. Another night, I dreamt of all of them with their hands and eyes tied and a cloth in their mouths, stuffed in sacks made of goat wool, just as I imagined

---

[21] The Eagle Stone

the girl kidnapped by the bandits who cast lots for whoever would get to marry her.

When I reached our gate, where the girls of the neighbourhood would gather, their song seemed very distant, longing, covered with a dusting of snow like wheat flour for a wedding, and the four verses that our Teacher had written on the board, when he was talking to us about Albanian traditions came to my mind:

Shtatë porta Bukojne
Shtatë porta parajse,
Aty ku lulëzojnë
Mrekullitë prej vajze.[22]

Girlish miracles...the miracles of girls...the miracles...'Hey, people, villagers...Do not forget, tomorrow at lunch, there will be a big conference for the action! Not in the council, but at the Burnt Mosque, tomorrow at lunch ...'

It was Craple announcing for the village. Did you hear that? Hear ye, hear ye: tomorrow at lunch, at the mosque...Nobody should be absent, as the "heavy" ones from the committee will come...

He went further and repeated these words several times, not only in the centre of the Upper Neighbourhood, but near each group of houses, where he thought that he had not been heard. He did so the entire evening; I went after him to the other neighbourhoods and watched the people listening to the crier. They looked at him from a distance, cautious not to get closer as if he had come from another world. At lunch...at the Burnt Mosque...Going back home, I stopped at the mosque...The scaffold, where they had put the murdered bear, was still in front of it...'The heavy ones from the committee will come,' Craple shouted. This is what was said to those who came from the committee to deal with the affairs of the village. Perhaps it was the distortion of the word important by the committee and Craple called them heavy[23].

Never had I heard of a conference being held at the Burnt Mosque. Someone must have chosen it for some purpose; perhaps to gather more people, because the square there was wider. There, we also played with beads or dice and coins from the king's time and cartridges left over from the last war. The bear's scaffold was also there, to remind people not only of the soft belt, but also of the

---

[22] Seven Bukojna gates/ Seven Eden gates/The place where/ girlish miracles thrive

[23] Heavy: i rëndë; important: i rëndësishëm

fire that had burned down our beautiful mosque overnight three years ago. From that day forth, it was called the Burnt Mosque. Its first name was scorched in flames and covered in ashes.

12

It was one of the most beautiful mosques in the province. Among the forty built by Sinan Pasha of Kallabak, ours and that of Prizren were said to be the most fine-looking, perhaps because nobody had ever seen the other thirty-eight, scattered as they were in Turkey, Yemen and Azerbaijan. When the flames hit the roof, many villagers tried to put out the fire but could not, even though the village's largest fountain was very close to the mosque. The mosque, the fountain and the bear scaffolding seemed to mark the three corners of a triangle and within there was the square where we played and where, the following day at midday, the "heavy" of the committee would bring the village together to take all the girls. It was said that Sinan Pasha himself had chosen the site of the mosque just because of the good water of Topillo.

One morning, many years after Sinan Pasha's remains in Anatolia had decomposed, all that was left from that beautiful mosque were the blackened walls and the grey ashes in the middle, just where the men used to pray and where I had heard the story of sacrifice. I loved the story about God commanding one of his servants to come down from heaven and bring that man a ram to sacrifice, so that he did not slaughter his only son. To me, God seemed better than the blind Homer of the Greeks who—as Teacher told me—three thousand years before Muhammad, had not managed this, but had slaughtered a girl so that favourable winds could blow over the sea. Anyway, from that day on, whenever I remembered Homer, he seemed to me like God himself, sitting on a celestial rock, in long garments, with a white and soft beard and a distant and ancient voice like that of Majka. There was only one difference between my Homer and the Lord in my mind; God looked after the world and its affairs, whereas blind Homer said to God, 'better be blind, because there is nothing to see in that world of yours, as You have let it become.' When these words came to my mind, I imagined Homer with a cut off tongue, just like that of Majka's great-grandfather, so that he would not commit heresy.

Many were the rumours that would circulate about the mosque's arsonist. Some said that it was Salko who wanted to boast in the committee; others mentioned another boy who had done this to get along well with Stalin and be accepted into the organisation; mostly it was talked inaudibly about a thief in the village who had stolen the carpets of the mosque and, to cover his tracks, had set it on fire. One of those who had gone to the capital swore that he had seen the carpets of our mosque in the marketplace of Milot, where he had stopped to have coffee at Marie Lulpali's. Others swore that the mosque was accidently set on fire by two soldiers who, on a cold winter night, lit a fire to warm themselves; some blamed an imam in the village who had not yet taken *"berat"*[24] to become a hodja, even though he had studied in the Madrasa of Prizren, while the one who had taken *"berat"* did not even know how to read the Koran well; some young people, who wanted to joke, had said that the fire was spread by the imam's cat, as he threw it on the brazier with burning charcoal because it would sneakily eat his eggs, and it caught on fire in the brazier and burned the whole mosque down. Still people, among themselves, quarrelled more over what someone had said carelessly: the mosque was burned down by Sinan Pasha's great-grandson, out of anger that he did not build it in his village, but in Bukojna. And there were people willing to die on this hill.

Only Majka's opinion differed from others'…'The curse followed Sinan Pasha here as well,' she said. 'The curse…Sinan Pasha…What strange things this Majka says! When I heard her talking like this, it seemed to me that she had already been born when the tongue of her great-grandfather or great-great-grandfather was cut off. In the following three years since the mosque was burned, the curse of Sinan Pasha that Majka told me of had constantly occupied my mind, especially on the days she took me to the Village of the Priest to heal. Riding the mule and rocking lightly on the saddle, she spoke as if talking to herself and explained the curse. It is a curse to leave your own child with no food, and, instead, feed others. Three times more cursed is the father who loses his children's bread in gamble. So is the one who beats up his son in the middle of the village for the others to see. But a thousand times more cursed is the pasha who kills the son to coddle the sultan, wherever and whoever he is! Damn you! Damned be your root and branch, your seed and family! Damned be the sun that warmed you and the moon that watched you, Sinan Pasha of Kallabak…Damned…Damned…The curse followed him even to this village of

---

[24] Authorization

51

ours…It follows him even now, hundreds of years after his bones melted, who knows where, under those yellow sands…'

'God, help us dodge this curse,' Majka whispered, unaware that I was looking at her lips and eyes to make out what she was saying.

13

Sinan Pasha heard that voice for thirty years. Thirty long years! It would haunt him in bed and on the table, in war and in the harems of the Sultan, in carouses and orgies. Every night—moonlit or not—he had heard this voice and that old woman had appeared to him, only as big as a handful of soil, but whose curse could shake the mountains…He closed his ears, shut the doors and windows of the palaces, but the curse came in anyway.

'Did her words find me?' he asked himself. Oh, no, he had taken the curse along with him. It was grinding his bones and sucking his blood dry. Probably since the day when a wolf ate his cattle and he searched for its burrow for seven days and took its cub. What was I thinking when I took it, just so I could boast in front of the other shepherds. He was the youngest among them and no one before him had ever caught a wolf cub. And where did that idea of taking it to the village alive come from! Take it away boy, a wolf at home is a curse; it breaks into the soul and you become wolf-hearted! You will roar around the world like a dire wolf in winter.

'Did it start then?' Sinan Pasha would ask himself. Or was it later, when I went down to the fields of Thessaloniki to overwinter the cattle? The Sultan's large army passed through those fields and no one made a sound, not even the mountain birds. But this was not the case for the herding dogs. Sinan had forty dogs to guard two thousand sheep. The dogs rushed to the Sultan's general and they would have torn him apart if he had not called them. When the dogs stopped waiting for his commands, the general called out: 'How did you stop forty dogs with two words?'

'They are Sinan's dogs and not the Sultan's *murtats*[25],' he replied. 'You come with me! I have cattle to guard,' he answered. 'Let the cattle be. The empire will be yours! You commanded forty dogs with two words; you can command

---

[25] Apostate

an entire army and become a great general, even greater than I…He was the son of the Sultan; Sinan was the son of a shepherd.'

They took him tied in ropes to make a general of him. It was then when his curse began. He fought in every corner of the empire, until he made a name for himself and the Sultan promoted him to the rank of general. 'Now go,' he told him, 'to command your people as you did with the dogs when you were a mountain shepherd.' 'Command my people like my dogs?' Sinan's blood boiled, but to him, it felt thick…soiled. A shepherd's blood, a wolf's blood, or a general's blood? None of the three and all three together. He took the decree and left…With a decree in his hand and a curse in his soul, he returned to our lands.

Get away you evil old woman! Was it my fault, or your son's? Why did he rebel against the Sultan? Then…when war begins, that's how it goes. Did you hear what your son said to the governor of our Sanjak? Or did you write the song yourself to embolden others too? Come on, tell me…

Pritmë, Hurshit Beu, pritmë,
Në ta zënça dot pusinë
Gjakun të kam për të pirë,
Veshkën me dy fije brinjë…[26]

What kinds of songs do these people make! Wild, like the abysses they inhabit. Ah, so it is the fault of my people? Hurshit Bey asked for three hundred eggs from each household, three hundred rams from each district and 300 girls from the provinces he ruled. He also abducted three hundred boys to be brought to Istanbul as janissaries. If I were there, I would also stand up to defend my sister who was being kidnapped by the Sultan's soldiers.

They caught Hurshit Bey, hung him on a plane tree by his feet, not his head, lit a fire below him and let it burn until he died. They humiliated him, killed him with his head down and his ass up. This revenge angered the Sultan tremendously, and he ordered Sinan to make his people obey as he had done with his dogs long before. That's what happened; he came and caught the rebelling son of the old woman, who later cursed him. Could the other generals know the hideaways of Albania? He caught him alive and, of course, he asked Hurshit Bey's mother about the punishment to be inflicted on the rebellious boy. Roast

---

[26] Wait for me, Hurshit Bey, wait,/ If I ambush you /I will drink your blood, /The kidney along two ribs

him alive, on a spit, she said. And everybody knows it so. The Sultan knows it so, too...

Yet they could not burn the rebellious boy alive. As soon as he learned of the punishment that Hurshi Bey's mother demanded, he asked his fellow prisoners to kill him, and they granted him his wish. Dead as he was, he was put on a spit over the embers, to say that they fulfilled the wish of the old woman and his majesty, the Sultan. Those who carried out the order were all murdered, so that they would not tell the truth.

* * *

The mule stopped by the side of a fence to get a mouthful of grass, and Majka continued her story. It is here, in my head, the voice of poor Sinan...

How light is this curse of yours, you old woman of Albania. You know nothing about what scorches my soul and what burns inside me! And you will never ever find out. If you knew, you would curse neither the sun nor the moon, just me and me only. And do you know what the most vicious curse would be? May you work for the Sultan, O Sinan! This would be the darkest malediction of all to me: the curse I received as a blessing the day I was first promoted. Man avoids curses as much as he can, but he is never afraid of blessings, until the blessing turns into a curse. May you work for the Sultan, O Sinan! I have worked for forty years. Worked...if you could call it work? Burn villages; kill boys so that they would not grow to rebel; kidnap girls, fill bags with gold, burn and kill again, and get promoted...When I caught your son, I was made Pasha! You, with no son, and I, a Pasha! But ranks fall, the curse remains...Now the Sultan is waiting for me...He has called me on an unusual day. The moon looks ominous...I am used to being summoned by the Sultan, even the ones preceding the one who is waiting for me today. Behold, he'll send his officer to take me.

That's what we did, when we thwarted the ploy of the nine pashas. The fools trusted me and revealed their plan. Yet, the very same day, they were summoned one by one and I cut off the heads of the nine at the feet of the Sultan. Our Sinan had been in the wars of the Empire, with them all. When he was about to behead the first, he reminded Sinan that together they had subdued Tripoli, Erzurum, and Aleppo of Syria. With the second, they had conquered Damascus. The third he beheaded was Kilic Pasha, along whom he had invaded Tunisia. With the fourth, they had surrounded the Castle of Halk-al-Wadi and he was the one who

55

saved him from a cunning ambush. He was sorry for the fifth. They had marched together over Georgia, but could not annex it, and the Sultan exiled them both to Didymoteicho. They shared soup for several months. They were saved by the women of the Palace, who loved that handsome pasha, and the ten thousand ducat bribe. With the sixth, they had spent the winter in Belgrade, after the Hungarian campaign…Together they burned Zemun and exhumed the remains of Saint Sava and threw them on the Danube. He did not strike the seventh on his neck, but split his head in two. He, together with Sinan's cousin, Ferhad Pasha, conspired against him and had him exiled to Malkara, but when the Sultan changed, Sinan also changed his place and, from exile, he came back as the head of the army. Along the last two pashas he slaughtered, he had made Yemen surrender, one of the greatest battles of his life…Following, he became Grand Vizier!

But the day came for the Sultan to summon him to the conspiracy room as well. Is it my turn? Will I slaughter or will I be slaughtered? Nobody knows…nobody understands…You leave for paradise and end up in hell…You leave as a pasha and you come back a *rayah*[27]. I don't know, I don't know…it seemed as if a quince-like thing had gotten stuck in his chest and was suffocating him…Whatever God provides; may He have mercy on His slave!

Sinan Pasha was standing by the big window of the palace, waiting for the Sultan's order, when he saw Hizir Pasha pass by…

He is going to his palace and does not even glance at my windows. Well done; that would add to my rage. You, old woman, you can at least sing for your son. What about Hizir Pasha and me? What can we say about our sons?

Hizir Pasha's son did not see the sun. Gone on a moonless night. Like the night that is coming to me. The night of your curse…What has my son done to annoy the Sultan?

This Hizir is also from our parts. Sinan's soldier, at first. Then he promoted him. Again and again. The more he killed, the more ranks he was given. So did the Sultan with him. Thorns grow from rain, ranks from blood.

When Sinan was about to promote him to a higher rank, he tested him. Neither his bravery nor his savagery, but his trustworthiness. He called him on his wedding day, before entering the bridal bed. He made him stay away for forty days, and at the end of the forty days, he sent him to fulfil a mission near his

---

[27] Tax-paying lower class of the Ottoman Empire, mostly referring to the non-Muslim subjects

village. But he also put people to follow him. The Pasha had ordered him not to trespass his house threshold to keep the order secret. But he violated it. He spent half of a night with his bride. 'Did you visit your bride?' Sinan Pasha asked. 'No, General!'

'Even if you did, it would not be a great sin,' he told him. 'No, General, I am happy to fight for you and for the Sultan.'

'Also for these,' he told them, and promoted him anew.

After nine months, his wife was about to give birth. Sinan ordered for her to be brought to the headquarters. The poor woman came with an enormous belly! He also summoned Hizir, who did not grow pale. His blood boiled. Tell me, Hizir, was it you to betray me or was it your wife to betray you? Will you allow me to tell the truth, Pasha? He shook his head to grant permission; he was not prepared for what the brave man caught in the trap he had set for him would do. Fast as a fox, he drew his sword and tore the woman's belly apart. 'This was not my child,' he said, also cutting off her head. Sinan Pasha had witnessed thousands of murders, but only this one frightened him, and he did not leave the headquarters' tent for two days. On the third day, he gave more ranks to the murderer of his own child…This is the great curse, old woman of Albania! Woe on him who this curse befalls, the curse of ranks!

And it is bizarre how a curse strikes, always unalike. Sinan had a friend; their path united them. The first, a shepherd in the mountains of Albania, the other broke stones in Karabakh. One was taken from the sheep, the other from the stones. One made dogs hush; the other carved stones and made them sing. They were put in the same room. 'Where are you from?' Sinan asked. 'Karabakh,' said the other. 'Me, Kallabak,' Sinan said. This is the name of one of the mountains where I went as a shepherd, at first. And so they became friends. Kallabak and Karabakh! The war never separated them. They were together when they set Armenia on fire. They scorched Bulgaria and Crete, side by side. They charred Illyria, also, hand in hand. They were promoted to Pasha on the same day.

It is unknown why the Pasha of Karabakh thought of giving that kind of gift to the Sultan. His curse followed him. He had a beautiful castle on the shores of the Black Sea and invited his Majesty there. He was aware of the sovereign's taste and pleased him with all drinks, meats, Karabakh quail and Armenian fruit. He finally took the Sultan to the big room, where he had gathered the forty prettiest girls of the Caucasus. 'They are more beautiful than the angels of Paradise,' the Sultan said. 'I have gathered them for you as if collecting dew from roses, O my Sovereign.' My poor father did not know about all the pleasures of the Sultan. Fighting for the great has no end. Being killed and killing again is not enough. Being burnt and burning is too little. 'Beautiful as the dew of roses, my Pasha,' the Sultan said. 'What about the rose?'

'Excuse me, my Sovereign?'

'Bring me the rose of your Palace …' The girl was only 17 years old and the Sultan had asked for her. The only daughter of the Pasha of Karabakh. Only he and the good Lord know what his soul endured at that moment. He did not utter a word, but went and took the girl by the hand and led her to the Sultan in the room; he himself went to the shore of the sea to drown the sighs under the grey waves. The sea made him turn grey, too. The sea roared, but the roar of the land surpassed the misery of the sea. The whole city was crying and screaming. They ran towards the castle. The daughter of the Pasha of Karabakh had thrown herself from the castle walls and was lying on the ground as a white and bloodstained rose. He was late; others took the girl in their arms. He heard the curses…To the Sultan or himself? From that day on the castle's name changed, never again was it called the Sultan's Castle, but the Girl's Castle. Maybe this is what it will be called for eternity…

A girl dared not to accept the Sultan! But how many were the pashas and generals that kissed his feet at any given moment? What kind of blood flows through their hearts…the blood of the powerful; they kill, burn, deceive, plunder, kill again, poison, betray friends, brothers, family, and children to earn a smile from the one above them, to climb even a little higher…'*Well now all this rambling is futile*,' Sinan thought. Death seems to be the savage wisdom of understanding life, of understanding oneself, to feel the muck in which you got or were placed in. The stench of muck has suffocated everything.

The mule stopped again for a mouthful of fresh grass.

And so, son, the Sultan summoned him. Your son wants to kill me, Sinan, he said. Along with several other officers. Your son's behaviour, Sinan, has gotten out of hand. What was Sinan Pasha, poor Sinan of Kallabak, to do?

When they gave him the *firman*, he went completely mad…

Conspiracy against the Sultan…My only son, associated with the conspirators. O Lord, what a curse! When he approached the Sultan, he smelled a foul odour coming from his ear. News of death came through that ear.

The Sultan ordered for Sinan's son to be brought. They brought him. Tied in dungeon chains. The rings in Sinan's neck clicked; he drew his sword, and did not see what he did or how he did it. They threw a bucket of water to wake him. He started shouting: I murdered him…I slew him…Oh, Mother, I beheaded my only son. I murdered my son! And the Sultan is alive!

And his pashas are also alive, here, snickering over my son's head…O Lord, release all the wrath of heaven on me and burn me alive! I slew my son, oh God! But why did they push him in front of me…just there, between me and the Sultan. Here is your conspirator, Sinan Arnaut[28]! Here you have him…Here you have him…Where do I have him? Where did he go? His head flew to the feet of the Sultan…Throw it in muck. Is this what he said? This is what he said, I guess…in muck…Where to? Where? My son's head in muck?

He frantically ran to his shepherd's hut, tried to put on his old clothes, but they didn't fit anymore. '*Not even my clothes accept me anymore,*' he thought. 'Yes, yes, these are my clothes. But I am also a stranger to my clothes, a stranger…a stranger to this world…At first, he would miss his village, the mountain, the lambs, the sound of the stock's bell. Then, they were all gone and forgotten. In wars and dumps. Kill and forget, kill and curse. And one day, the curse will befall. It seems as if it forgot you, but it is there within you, like a wolf in its skin.'

'Ah, who will take me out of the pit I have fallen in, from this filthy abyss where I have entered whole, heart and soul, body and mind?' exclaimed Sinan. Oh deepest layer of hell, you could never be blacker than this day of mine, a thousand snakes slither through my body, a thousand witches grab me by the throat, a thousand fires burn my eyes…I killed him, with these hands and with this sword!

Curse, curse and never cease the cursing! What else do you want from me, you cranky old lady of Arnautistan[29]? I killed your son; I killed mine too! I killed them both for the Sultan! Got it, I killed them for the Sultan! Yours to obtain ranks, mine to keep them. Happy now? I killed my son too…I killed my own son…

He came out of the Sultan's Palace walking on the ruins of his life. The word had left his mind. Tears had left his eyes. His heart was separated from his soul, and he could not even mourn his son, whom he himself murdered. No one went to comfort him. Just a knowledgeable and wise imam from our sides: 'Sinan,' he told him, 'you killed your own son for wealth and ranks. With the ranks and the

---

[28] Albanian

[29] Land of Albanians

gold that you have gathered, build forty mosques around the world to cleanse this barbarity of yours…Otherwise, you will wander around the world like a ghoul, with no name nor mark.' He took his advice and built forty mosques. He raised this one of ours too, smaller, but just as beautiful as the one in Prizren…But the curse also followed him here…Sinan Pasha of Kallabak was also burnt down here…

14

Unlike on other occasions, women were present in the conference as well. Majka, Nefka, another woman whose name nobody in the village knew and whom even her own husband referred to as "she". Two or three others from the lower neighbourhood were also there. Çinarçe's wife had also come, probably for fear of being registered for action. She had heard that, at one of the previous conferences, her husband asked whether he could send his Versije to action, which meant comfort—for some time—without her. They had all pulled their headscarves and white cloths over their foreheads so that their eyes were not seen, and they only did this when there were strangers in the village. I had occupied a corner from where I could see but could not be spotted—not to mention that nobody really cared about me. Everyone was watching the delegates who were sitting on some bench-like seats brought from the school; they had also placed a table for those of the organisation and the village council. I was struck by the one who looked like the "heaviest" among the delegates, wearing military trousers, boots and an unbuttoned jacket so that the gun tucked into his belt was seen. He stood up first and said something I could not hear, yet I saw him shake both hands at once, then wag his index finger and raise his voice, but his words still did not reach my ears. He would sit and stand whenever a villager spoke or asked a question. To me, the men of the village looked sombre, as if they had been soaked in a pot with walnut shells[30].

I can't say for how long this went on; it seemed like it had been hours when I noticed that it was getting dark, partially because dusk was approaching and partially because of the March fog of that year. I tried to get closer and listen better when Olloman America got up to speak. I came to learn much later that, even though he bore that name, he had never been to America. Apparently, it had been given to him because, unlike the others, he wore a fedora hat like those of

---

[30] Clothes are boiled with walnut shells to dye them brown

the Al Capone era; he was the only villager who dug his garden with a spade; and also the only one who, when the village cows came out to graze and roamed the streets, followed them with a large bag, collected the dung and took it to his garden. Somebody once mocked him regarding the dung issue: it is unbecoming for America to collect what cows excrete, but he cut it short: work is what made America, America…He had no one and lived alone. His sons had left and settled somewhere in Mostar, Bosnia; they had also taken their mother with them, but he had refused to go. If they were in America, he would have probably been tempted, but there was nothing for him elsewhere. Even when he entered the café, he stayed alone in a corner, drinking one or two teas and not chatting with anyone. He was the tallest man in the village, but he looked even bigger when he stood up to speak, probably also because of the spot he had occupied nearby the ruins of the mosque. Everyone looked at him in bewilderment, not only because he was known as a quiet man, but also because he had no daughter to send to the action.

'I have a question,' he said, 'why are the girls of our village the only ones being asked to go? Are they the finest, the most hardworking, or is it because they have no brothers?'

'This is a great honour for our village,' Salko replied, shaking the bench he was sitting on.

'A great honour, Stalin, a great honour, indeed. But why don't you also honour the Locality from where there are people both in the committee with a balcony and in the committee without one. Its people are in Security and education, in the police force and far away in the government? Or is it because they come as delegates and we're desolate?'

An electrifying murmur pervaded the crowd. I got even closer; no one would bother to look at me, so I made myself comfortable under the bear scaffold, from where I could hear and see better. When Olloman told the delegates not to ill-treat us and not to toy with us like a dog does with a mat, I heard a thunderbolt I don't know which of the delegates released:

'This is what only enemies of the state say!'

'Ah, if so, I speak no more, because the spoon has burned my lip with all the governments that have passed over my back. They are like Zhupa's bride, the first winter a rabbit, the second a fox and the third a wolf. I have no money to buy trouble, therefore I am leaving because I have no daughter for the action,' Olloman America said, and set out to leave the crowd where he was.

'If you have no daughter, why did you come in the first place?' shouted Nefka, who held a grudge against him since the day when they quarrelled over their grandfathers' bones.

'Did you come to spit venom and run away?'

'Sit and explain yourself,' the delegate insisted.

'Explain what? I only have dung.'

He pulled his fedora over his head and left. The people could not stand still. The delegates spoke without taking turns and nobody managed to understand whether they were quarrelling with the villagers or among themselves. I saw Teacher get up and ask permission to speak. Silence fell.

'It's not fair to interpret the words of the people negatively. People need to be clarified for the sake of the action; the girls will go and learn. They will also go by my Shkodra; it is a good thing. But why do it shouting? Which Olloman will overthrow the state? His name may be America, but he is not America. Just like this secretary who is called Stalin, but he is not Stalin, is he?'

'Do not mess with me,' Salko growled, 'and do not throw Olloman's dung into my pie.'

'Olloman spoke the truth, let girls from other villages come too...' Teacher went on. Thunders again: 'Who are you to teach us? Teach the kids; the state has its own teachers...' All the delegates said something against Teacher, but the gravest of them all was what the main delegate said:

'Do you know who brought you here?' He asked. 'You did,' Teacher replied awkwardly.

'No, not me, your father did. Your father brought you, but we will talk about this another time. Now sit down, because this village does not concern you.' I noticed that Teacher was tense. He sat down, shut up, and put his head between his knees...what else could be done in the face of that yawp? With a trembling voice, he said: 'This village concerns me for as long as I am the teacher of these mothers' and fathers' children, who I thank for the respect they have shown me, and I have not bothered anyone...'

'But there is a big burden on your back, so try not to make a mess of this important gathering of the people. Who are you to embosom them?' said the main delegate, who would have continued, had some shouts not been heard from behind the charred wall of the mosque. A group of seven or eight girls came out, stood by one of the still undemolished corners of the wall and let out the words, which fell like lightning in the half-darkness of that March. 'Either all, or none!

Why only from Bukojna? Let the engaged ones come with us, too! Who will accompany us? Either all, or none! Why must we be treated like red-headed stepchildren…What about Saint George[31], will you take us back to the village?' They all spoke at once and took a step forward in each demand.

'You will go hoping and skipping!' yelled Salko, rising up. The main delegate grabbed him by the jacket and in a menacing tone told him: 'You sit there!' But when the girls went on, he himself rose to his feet, and the others followed.

'Everybody go home, only the parents of the girls that shouted stay here,' said the "heaviest" of the delegates. When they heard these words, the girls ran away like birds, frightened by a rifle's shot or by the greyhound's barking. The hunter had shot their shelter. When there were only five men left, the team leader said fiercely: 'Go get your wives and daughters, and come to the Council! Clear? Clear!'

---

[31] May 6th is Saint George's Day and it is traditionally celebrated with flowers

15

The desolation of the mosque covered the village in its entirety. The five men that remained there did not know what to say or do; stay or leave, while the delegates set off to the households, where they were ordained to dine and spend the night. The chief summoned Salko and ordered him to go to the border post and tell the commander to send two soldiers to guard the parents of the rebel girls. Keep them all night and, when we arrive we only want one name: the name of who organized the protest.

I was the last to leave the shelter where I hid, and only then did I realise what the odour that filled my nose and chest had been. It was the smell of the killed bear that had not been removed yet...

In the morning, no one had the time to bother with the men, who spent the whole night locked in the Council offices; the whole village awoke in the bed of fear from news that rolled through every street and gate as an enormous pointed stone falling from Maja e Zezë[32]: a dog had bitten the chief of the committee team. Which, who, whose, was it not tied, who untied it, where did it see him? Plenty of other questions rolled from one window to another, from one street to another, as people stretched their heads around the corners to hear something. The worst part was that the order had been to keep the village dogs tied even at night, when the team arrived, what was very uncommon, because at night all the dogs were untied and they wandered around the houses until the morning to guard or at least to somehow announce the approach of a stranger, whoever he may be.

'The team is afraid even of dogs,' Mother said when she heard the order.

'Will we also tie Dudan?' I asked.

'Why tie it?' Mother replied. 'Dudan is not a chain dog. He bothers nobody.'

---

[32] The Black Peak

'What about the order?' said Father thoughtfully, 'The order is for those that bite.'

'How would the team know whether they bite or not; we could end up in trouble, in vain.'

'We don't tie Dudan at day time, why tie him at night?' Mother attacked. These words seemed to convince Father, and we didn't tie him up overnight. We had not tied him up even on the night of the calamity. The whole village knew my dog, because no other dog's hair was white as a lamb's like his was.

It was a troubled night, and as if in a daze, I recalled bits of the conference at the Burnt Mosque, Teacher's words, the chief's yawp, the girls' cries, and even Majka, who did not open her mouth for hours, but kept watching the charred mosque stones, as if she was living in another world and seemed not to hear what was being said and who was talking around her. The next day, while the five villagers were still locked in the Council, she went to the mosque with tongs, a trowel, a bunch of celosia and a jug in hand. She filled the jug in Topillo and slammed the tongs and trowel, spraying the burnt stones with water, soaking the handful of celosia and shaking it in the air. Occasionally, she would stop and whisper words only she knew, lowering and raising her head three times towards the sky and spitting lightly, as if she had someone in front of her. I did not talk to her until she was done, for I knew that if I spoke, the spell would be broken. She had taught me this herself. 'Yet, you mustn't engage with these things, all times have their own magic, your magic is school,' she would often tell me.

'What are you doing, Majka?' I asked when she was finished.

'I am blowing the curse away, so that it leaves our village. The curse of Sinan Pasha wanders through these walls and ruins; he is destroying our village's life.' She had not yet finished her words, when a woman passed by and, vicious as she was, cried out: 'You blow in vain, o sorceress, in vain! One calamity after the other is befalling us. Have you heard that a dog bit the head of the team, and they are summoning all the men in the basement?'

These words seemed to tear my chest apart. '*Our dog was the only one that was not tied up last night,*' I thought. Did Dudan bring this disaster upon us? On my way to the Council, I heard someone calling to another across the street. 'It was the white dog to bite him, the white dog.' O God, Dudan, what have you done to us? Those who had gathered at the Council did not speak. Whose is the white dog? Gather all the dogs here; go get them from your houses or wherever you hid them. The team chief walked ferociously from one corner of the council yard to the other and shook the bound hand the dog had bitten. 'Did you or didn't you hear? Bring the dogs here, so we can find that bastard!' the post commander shouted. 'Not necessary, I am the only one to own a white dog,' Father said. 'Bring it here, then,' the commander shouted. 'I will not hand over my dog,' Father replied. I was about to run to hide Dudan, but the commander's voice debilitated me. 'You won't hand it over, sir? You break the orders and act brave, right?'

'It's not a matter of bravery, but of tradition…the dog is one of the family', someone from the furthest rows spoke. 'You don't hand over the dog, and we burn the house along with the dog in it,' the commander said angrily. Father grew pale and gestured to me. I pretended not to understand, but when he repeated it, I headed home. I took Dudan, put the beautiful collar around his neck and left for the Council. The entire village had heard of the incident, and people had come out at most of the gates of the neighbourhood, as if they were seeing me off to another world. At some point, I heard a cry: 'Do not hand over Dudan!' I did not turn my head to see who spoke. When I took my dog to the Council, the chief said, 'Yes, it was this one.' Dudan was so quiet that I thought this had been fabricated to set us up. The crowd of villagers was bigger, and two or three soldiers of the border post had also arrived. They carried rifles.

'Tie it by the willow,' the commander ordered me.

'What, what are you doing?' Father cried. 'You will have to pass through me to kill that dog!' Dudan barked for the first and last time that morning. Two soldiers grabbed my father by his arms, while the commander pulled the revolver out of its holster and shouted: 'This is how anyone who tries to bite our new state ends up!' Two shots in a row seemed to blow my mind out, and it felt as if my head was empty, completely empty, like a pumpkin-jug. Dudan bumped onto the willow trunk and his white hair was crimson with blood. He whimpered twice or three times with a feeble voice, and then made no other sound. The villagers were bewildered; their mouths were dry and they could not speak. Father tried to take the killed dog, but was stopped by the voice of the team chief: 'Leave it there, until everyone sees it. Go and call the school pupils along with all the teachers!' A young woman, a member of the team, who had not opened her mouth once during the conference of the previous day, left the council yard saying:

'This is no good, Comrade Hasip.'

I did not move from my spot. Most of those who came to see the murdered Dudan passed by in silence. Only Olloman America told someone:

'They thought that they could find a village without a dog.'

'Look at what they did!' the other said.

'Eeh, this is how this will go,' Olloman replied. 'A bad dog brings the wolf to the sheepfold; the good one brings the government.' Three hours later, we took Dudan and I wanted to bury him in a patch by the yard, but Father didn't allow me.

He put him in a sack and threw it in a ravine at Përroi i Madh[33].

In the evening, the conference was convened again. It did not last more than twenty minutes. Only those who had daughters of age for action were present. 42 men in total. All crestfallen. No speeches were held.

'So, who wants to speak?' asked the chief of the team, Hasip Disha. Nobody expected the imam of the village to be the first to stand up. 'Sign my two daughters up,' he said and sat down. 'We will not start the list with your daughters, imam,' called the youth secretary of the village. 'Write my sister's name first.'

'All right, boy, after you,' murmured the imam. Thirty-one people signed to have their daughters sent to action. The youth secretary read the names. 'The eleven ones left will sign tomorrow,' the chief said and the conference was dismissed.

The men of the village did not move, as if they had forgotten where to go. They looked at each other and whispered the words that Olloman America had once said: 'Traj i tërpi, fetvo kërpi,' and Teacher had translated as if it were a rhyme: 'Silent and patient, mend the rags!'

---

[33] the Great Stream

16

But the following day, it was the case of a sudden death, and all the men of the village set off for the city. The bridge on Drin had collapsed and one of the dead was from our village; he had just sold two baskets of winter pears, dug in the straw, in the marketplace, and, as he was crossing the bridge, death struck him…For twelve hours, the men of the village carried the body in a made-up stretcher, a carpet and two long beech groves. All those who met them and asked what had happened received the very same answer, regardless of which of the men spoke on behalf of all:

'He died in the city, at the bottom of the bridge.'

It was said that the blow came from below, from the roots of the bridge. A terrible noise, like the breaking of black pine logs in legends, was heard. Then there was a bewildering shake and those who happened to be on the bridge fell into the river waters, alongside large chunks of concrete.

The first of the four drowned to be pulled out was our villager. He had clenched his jaw a little and a stream of blood slid from his temple, by the ear, to reach his neck. In his left hand, he was clutching the rope of the halter, which, had it not been torn, might have saved his life, as the mule would have pulled him along.

Then a boy and a girl were pulled out. As they were being brought to the shore, a scream, which seemed to cut the river in half, was heard.

'Martin, Brother!'

A young woman had run away from the crowd a bit further and was about to get into the river. She hurried and was not aware that she was walking in water, until some youngsters managed to stop her.

The people were frozen. The image of the collapsing bridge foot was already engraved in their retinas, yet no one was leaving. The last to come was the Dervish of Kolsh. Every day he entered the waters of Drin, in a white shirt and underwear, he spoke to the river and to the Lord, but the people did not listen to him. Familiar with his story of a murder within the family, they did not disturb him, nor did they listen to his words. But on that day, everybody expected something. As if a mind disturbed by the bloodshed within his household would say what many normal minds could not?

The Dervish of Kolsh plunged his hands in the river several times, spoke unheard words to the turbulent waters several times and then raised his hands to the sky, shouting: 'This bridge is cursed! Cursed!' Everyone was stunned and turned their eyes to the demolished bridge. The dervish came out of the river and left without uttering a word. Droplets of water trickled from his white shirt, long hair and black beard, leaving some strange marks on the dusty road.

Later on, everybody understood the truth in the Dervish's words. The bridge had been blown up during the war and rebuilt after. It was built by the very same German engineer, a certain Irving Hartman, who had blown it up a few weeks ago. He was taken hostage and brought to the bridge. Once he was finished, many people came to cross the bridge; two partisans had put the German engineer in the middle. People cast curious glances at him, but he looked at the river only and seemed to speak to its grey waters. Two trucks carrying grain approached. They crossed the bridge, and it shook slightly, whereas Irving Hartman shivered from head to toe. He shouted something, but people didn't understand, because he spoke in his own language…And they did not pay attention to him. Recently, he had been talking to himself quite often and the people of the town would say that the German of the bridge had either gone or would go mad one of those days. But that time he could not stand the deafness of the people watching the bridge he built with his own hands. He shouted once more, aloud, saying the same words. Then, in the blink of an eye, he put his foot on the railing of the bridge and jumped down.

When people reached out, they saw him crashing on the chunks of concrete still there from the time he himself had blown up the bridge. In a few seconds, the river took him away. His dead body was pulled out two hundred meters further. He was the last German to die in Albania.

Yes, but he was the demon of the river, those who knew better would say, he brought calamity after eleven years. He had devilishly calculated the flow of the river waters, and he rested the foot of the bridge not on sound rock, but on gravel. For eleven years, the river eroded the gravel and the foot of the bridge remained hanging in void until it collapsed…While sketching his calculations, he had written: 'The bridge will be buried here, and this town will tremble from my curse!'

'The German's curse also befell us,' Majka said.

* * *

The killing of the dog had served its purpose. Four days later, the eleven girls who had initially refused, along with their families, were compelled to sign to go to action: some out of the desire to go a little beyond Gjallica, some out of the shame of being separated from their peers, and, all together, out of fear of those words repeated in every village, at every fountain where the girls gathered together to fetch water and tell the secrets of their age, in every furnace where bread was baked, on every fire where coffee was brewed, and by every hayloft where women took the last load of hay for that winter: that is, this is the fate of anyone who tries to bite our new state.

17

Six days later, the girls left for action. It was a bitter March morning, with the sun hiding behind a despairing fog. Yet, the whole village went to see them off. The Council had also paid Musa of Novoseja to come and escort them with drums and pipes…Starting from the very last house in the Lower Neighbourhood, the girls gathered at the square of the Burnt Mosque, from where they would depart. Musa played the pipes as if it were a wedding, but none of the girls danced, so he felt obliged to play a men's dance, which was danced by some young boys. I saw them all one by one; none of them had a sister going to action. But I was surprised by one among them, dancing with great joy. It was a man with hay-like hair who I recognised from the jacket he had on; he had also worn it the day before, when I saw him in the stockyard where I went to catch any dormant sparrows and as I was moving slowly as to not wake the sparrows, I heard a whisper, so I stopped and put my ear near a hole of the hayloft, woven with hazelnuts withes. The whispers came from inside. I reached the door and opened it quietly; I had become a master in this so that I wouldn't risk scaring the sparrows, not to mention humans whose hearing is duller than that of birds. I could not see anything in the darkness, but I heard two voices and their words petrified me. 'Will you come to meet me in action?' the girl asked. 'I could cross nine mountains on foot just to come to you,' the boy replied, 'I would turn into a bird just to come to you' and more hokum, which also made me blush in the dark.

'Don't tear my shirt,' the girl raised her voice. 'With what will I go to action?'

'And let the action tear it before me? I won't allow it!

Then I heard some strange noises, lips smacking, half-said words, sighs I had never heard before, and I felt numb and powerless. But I was even more scared by the thick voice of the boy, who started shouting like the scythe holders mowing in the mountain. I could not bear it anymore, so I ran away without catching any sparrows. I hid in a corner until the boy passed by, and it was the same debaucher that danced with all its might, with the same kersey jacket on, from which he seemed to not have yet shaken off the dry grass. I glanced at the girls to find out which one was mown last night, but they all stood crestfallen and did not even want to look at their peers jumping rampantly as they danced. The night before, once I saw the boy coming out of the hayloft, I did not wait to see with whom he was inside, amidst hay and sparrows. It seemed as if I would do something shameful; as if I would also be to blame. But in the morning I had a burning desire to find out who she was. I looked at them one after the other, and they reminded me of those cold-struck sheep that our shepherds took to the river before shearing and dumped in a place where the water is deeper, like a stone-built pool in the middle of the stream; they throw them several times until their hairs turn white and the poor sheep bleat in fear while the men grab them by the legs and toss them in the middle of the river-pool once, twice…five times…until they get tired and do not try to run away anymore. We, the little ones, were taken to the river to stay around the sheep to keep them from fleeing. That morning, too, we were standing like that, at the end rows of the crowd, waiting for the leader to move towards Vlahanica and take the long way to the city.

But time would not pass and nobody knew why. When Musa stopped playing and the boys stopped dancing, a whisper spread among the crowd: the two daughters of the imam have not come. 'We won't go without them,' I heard one of the girls say. Her voice sounded like the one I had heard last night, but in a moment, another spoke saying 'we will not wait for the imam's tricks forever,' and it also sounded like the voice of the hayloft girl, and, confused, I thought I was either ill or I had daydreamt.

We escorted the girls to Ribar, the last among the hills our village shares with the Orgosta meadows. The women sang farewell songs, which they made up on the spot and the girls cried. This is how I remember that parting, a mixture of tears and crying, of songs and words that at the time made no sense, as I did not understand to whom they were sung and what they advised the girls of.

Only when we went back to the village did we learn why the imam's daughters had not come; overnight the whole family had fled in a hurry to the other state. For sure, they had not let the action tear their shirts, I thought to myself in a rave…Pretty soon, a thousand and one versions of this flight spread throughout the village, what would you not hear and everyone was trying to get the wind blow at their back. The imam's house was a bit secluded from the village, built on his own land, with a garden. I noticed a group of men going there. Two were from the village Council, one from the Democratic Front, and a fourth was the school principal, also a member of the District Committee. First, they searched that part of the house where one of the imam's sons lived separately. They found an envelope nailed on the front wall of his room; on it was written: 'To be given to Zaim Rrashta, in the locality. Whoever is the first to find this letter and does not hand it to Zaim Rrashta but opens it, will pay for this with his life!' The deputy mayor, who had come to pick up the girls for the action, took the letter and gave it to the captain; then, from the locality centre, the police came. It made a list of every item in the house, while the belongings were given to the village council. When they were done, the inspectors went to the courtyard, took a beehive, and satisfied their sweet tooth with honey and the pancakes, a pan full of which the imam's wives had left on the table still laid. The news that they had thrown a pancake every four-five steps along the way to the border spread immediately. We, the hungry boys of the village, rushed there to eat any of the pancakes but found nothing; maybe it was a lie or maybe someone had finished them before we got there. Thus, nobody got to learn in which direction they had crossed: all those people, five men, seven women, three young girls, and a dozen of children, one of whom was still a baby in a cradle.

In the afternoon, the imam's belongings were transported to an empty building near the Council offices, the house of an earlier runaway, which was used to collect the belongings of the other runaways. Those who went to take the hodgepodge of the imam, found another letter on the back of the door to a room; it was opened and bore no life threats to those who read it. This one, apparently, was addressed to the villagers: 'Dear friends who will check my house, I am leaving my homeland, because I have been denied all my rights in this country. I built a mill on the Oreshka Bridge, Harun Demiri took it from me; I started to build another one on the Bukojna River, but I was not allowed to finish building it. Next, when all the people were summoned to the mosque to mourn Stalin and to swear allegiance to his line, I was expelled from the mosque, where my family served for generations with a white turban and pure spirit, and the *berat* for imam from Istanbul. This was very hard for me.' Maybe he had written more, but that's all the villagers came to learn.

The letter bore no name at the end, and it was not clear whether it was the imam or any of his sons to have written it. The second letter was also confiscated

74

by the captain, but the words in it had already been learned by the whole village. Many years later, the poor imam, who had not been allowed to mourn Stalin, would be asked to conduct the religious ceremony before King Zog's burial, in Paris. After going through numerous vicissitudes, from the refugee camp in Kaçanik onwards, he and his family fled to the neighbouring country, where he left his youngest son hostage, and settled in France, in a village near Paris. When the king died, our imam and all his sons attended the funeral. At some point, another imam approached him and asked: 'Where are you from?'

'From Albania,' our imam replied. 'It is better if the prayer is conducted by an imam from the country of the deceased,' said the unknown imam. 'These are the words of the Qur'an and I know them, but I did not know that among all the turbans gathered there, there was none from Albania.'

'No, we are from Egypt; the king's friends sent us.'

'Well, I came on my own; nobody sent me,' said the imam of my village, and took over directing the ceremony for the funeral of the first and last king of Albania. And just imagine that at a young age he had been imprisoned along with other opponents of the king and, by a strange coincidence, was put in the same cell with the writer of the novel "Sikur t'isha djalë"[34], with another young patriot from Kolonja, who translated Goethe's "Faust", and a third man, at the time not famous but who would later become one of the founders of the National Front. These were recorded in "Ditar nga burgu"[35] of the writer, the only book in Albanian that was found during the raid in the imam's house, and, since the police from the Locality threw it away as a worthless item, one of the Council members took it and it is preserved to this day by his grandsons.

---

[34] If only I were a boy

[35] Prison Diary

18

Enraged, I went through the seven gates of Bukojna, and as I was returning home, I saw Teacher standing by the open window of the room the Council had given him. He was staring afar at the mountains of Kollovoz and didn't notice me, but I kept waving, willing to have him greet me back. That day, school was off, and he had not left the house at all, not even to see the departure of the girls. When he noticed me, he signalled for me to enter and I went.

'Are you getting bored with no school?' he asked. 'I believe next year the seven-year school will be opened here as well and you will be back in the classroom.'

If only that day would come. The Committee Chairman had said that the school would be opened, but it was not. Teacher explained me that I should finish the seventh grade and then I would go to high school in the city, and, when my father and I sat together in the field to rest and give the oxen some hay to eat, he had told me that he was ready to even sell even his pillow to not leave uneducated. But it was about two years since I finished elementary school and wandered around the village, constantly feeling like a bag hanging on the porch which was blown to whichever direction the winds blew. Yet, I don't know why at that moment I had a burning desire to talk about something other than my schooling.

'I am more upset about the girls,' I told Teacher, 'I am afraid that they won't be given permission even on Saint George's Day, which is about a month and a half away, and they'll be in action for three or four months …'

'Maybe they'll be given permission for two or three days,' Teacher comforted me.

'Maybe, yet, without the girls, Saint George's doesn't count.' I said. 'It is as if God made it for them, at least in our village …'

'Don't the others celebrate it?'

'Everyone celebrates it, but the girls are the celebration in and of themselves. Without them, even the flowers hardly bloom. The children go to pick flowers in Govorusha and on Saint George's Day we put them in cauldrons and bathe in them. But the girls send flowers to their fiancés, or the boys they love. Have you seen that the boys pass by the gates, when the girls sing? It is there where love takes root with a bouquet a girl sends to a boy. The ones of Saint George are the first flowers; later, they plant white and pink carnations, violets, marigolds, lemon balm and many others in every corner of the garden, but none is like the flowers of Saint George! Then, the next day, you know what. The boy cut willows, some a branch and some a whole willow and decorate the gates of their girls with them; they compete to see who will have the biggest and most beautiful willow.'

'Have you ever cut any willows?' Teacher teased. 'Yesterday I got the first bouquet …' I pulled out of my pocket a handful of white, dried carnations. I flushed from tip to toe and did not understand why I was telling this to Teacher.

'Oh,' he wondered, 'who brought you them?'

'You know her, Teacher …have you heard that, three days before the departure for action, one of the girls got married, just so she'd not go? The wedding was set up, allegedly the fiancé kidnapped her and so on, but the Council did not buy the wedding trick; it made their father send his youngest daughter. Like myself, she is just thirteen.'

'Thirteen to action?'

'Yes! Yes! Go to fetch water for the others, they said. Your father can't deceive us, even if he marries off your mother,' Salko told her.

'And …?'

'And she left today …'

'Aha, I see,' Teacher said, 'is she the one who sat on the same desk as you?'

'Yes, it's her.' Teacher took me in his arms and started to stroke my hair.

'In the evening, before the action, she sent me carnations. They might be dry, but still, they are carnations.'

'Oh, what a girlish miracle!' He whispered and sat abruptly on his chair. He wrote something and gave it to me…

Shtatë porta Bukojne,
Mbetën shkret të shtatat,
Nuk dëgjohet kënga,

Iku bashkë me vajzat![36]

I read it several times and, when two tears fell on the paper, he took it from my hand and tore it. 'Don't tell anybody,' he told me. I went out and tried to recall those other verses of the Teacher on the gates and the girls...Seven Bukojna gates, Seven heaven gates, the place where girlish miracles flourish, heaven is gone...gone...gone...With every step I took, I said a gone...gone...heaven was gone...

---

[36] Seven Bukojna gates,/ deserted, the seven,/ no song to be heard,/ gone with the girls

19

When I went out the door of the house where Teacher lived, I almost bumped into my grandmother. She was leaving the house of Drango Donguzi—next door—a childless man, although he had married four times. I had never seen Grandma Ajnurka so distrait, exhausted and irate. 'Scum of the Earth!' she shouted enraged, not watching her steps. She bumped on a stone and almost broke her neck, but I managed to hold her. Only then did she realise I was her daughter's son.

'And you? You were sent by Lord, may His name be blessed! Let's get away from this scum, from this dirty scab!'

I was thinking about what could have gone on between my grandmother and Drango, but I did not understand the affairs of the adults, even when they were grandparents, uncles, or aunts. Perhaps an old debt he wouldn't give her back, I thought, as I held my grandmother by her arm for fear she would fall again. I knew that many men in the village were in debt to my grandmother, who had helped many people during the first, second and even this last famine—which had not been numbered yet—with the money her brother sent her from Sarajevo. Yet, I didn't believe that my grandmother would get so angry for a debt and keep shouting all the way home: scum…scum…scum…the most severe swear used by women for a man who deserved it. I didn't ask her, because I knew her nature: when she was angry, she didn't want to be asked or to answer. She explained things later, when she calmed down.

'And you, little scum,' she addressed me, 'why don't you ask me what the issue with that big scum was?'

I was shocked and didn't know what to say; even though it was her to urge me, I was still afraid to ask. Even though I was dying to find out what had happened, I didn't open my mouth. She turned to Drango's house and called:

'You won't be giving birth to shit, you scum, because neither your head nor your ass works! May your eyes blow out, and may your bones dry out!

This lightning in a clear sky that my grandmother released enlightened me for a moment and, after that, I was expecting the thunder to follow…'

Drango had divorced three wives, as they did not bear him children. But the fourth one was not conceiving either, so the villagers had started to make fun of him. 'He is as big as an ox, but furrows are not to be opened with a single pear shoot, and thus you can neither plant nor reap!' These words spread so extensively that he began not to go out into the village, neither for lunch and dinner, nor for Eid and the Great Night.

One day, he roared throughout the neighbourhood that Nefka and Ajnurka had cast a spell on his wife, so she'd not give birth and asked them both to go to his house, wash the woman with lemon balm with their own hands, so that the spell was washed away from her body. Nefka, who was related to him, went and washed her, but my grandmother refused. 'I don't know how to cast or uncast spells; I have never known and I don't wish to learn,' she said. 'He can take his wife to the Sheh of Grykë[37], if he feels like it.' The fame of this sheikh, who performed magic on women for two or three nights in his house, and they gave birth after nine months, had also reached our village. He undid spells, some would say. They said that the strongest magic he undid was that of a woman whose eleven children died because she had strangled a hen and its eleven chickens. The twelfth lived. Others said that he lowered his pants, so to speak.

Drango Donguzi eventually made my grandmother wash his wife, too. He waited for her to be home alone with her son's wife and the two little children and banged on their door vigorously.

'You either come to wash my wife now, or I will set the house on fire and make you miserable!

Left with no other choice, my poor grandmother went to deal with Drango's spells. While she washed the woman, he waited in the next room. When she was done, she called out at him:

'Now that your wife is washed and clean, take her to the Sheh of Grykë and after nine months your household is full. May the Sun spit on you, you scum!'

He came out like a raging ox and rushed to throw her down the stairs, but Grandma shook the cane she carried along and the man was taken aback. But since the day she washed his wife, my grandmother could not find peace…'The evil of shame is worse than the evil of pain,' she would tell me. 'He gave me a reputation as a magician. He put me in the same lot with Nefka. Dirty seed!'

---

[37] The Sheikh of the Gorge

20

Life had regaled my grandmother pain and big wounds over the years. Her first husband died and left her with a little daughter and she decided to never marry again, but from the very first year after his death she felt that her brothers and especially her sisters-in-law considered her to be a heavy burden; she was not worried for herself, but for the little girl who was seen not as a child of the family, but as an orphan taken from the streets. To eat, she was mostly given some leftover bones; to dress, she was given the old clothes of those who were older. Only the brother who was in Sarajevo would occasionally send something for his niece too. She was thoroughly fed up, when a woman from the Upper Neighbourhood came and asked to talk to her alone in a corner near the stack. 'Çaush wants to marry you,' she told her. 'He told me that...'

'Hmm, don't tell me what he told you, because I don't want to hear it from others; if he wants me to be his wife, tell him to come and talk to me tomorrow, at this spot, and tell him to bring the Koran along.'

The next day, he came with the holy book in his hand, unaware of what it could be used for at the haystack, where he would be talking about marriage with a young widow. For a moment he felt perplexed, remembering the ancient saying that advised not to trust winter nights, turbulent waters and the widowed women, and he considered going back, but in his uncertainty, he had already reached the haystack. This would also be his second marriage, as he had sent the wife away for some reason but had not allowed her to take along the daughter she had given birth to and had kept her at home. A man cannot raise a girl, relatives had told him, sooner or later you have to get married, so the sooner the better. He thought of Ajnurka and sent for her. He waited just a little at the haystack, flipping through the Koran, before she came.

'Listen,' Ajnurka told him, 'it was you to chase me and not the other way around; you have a daughter and so do I; your fireplace has no coal and mine is also cold; I come and light the fire and warm you for all the blessed life God bestowed us with, but on one condition: your daughter is mine and mine is yours. If they happen to find out that they have no mother or father, I won't stay with you for another minute.'

What he heard made his eyes open wide, but in the meantime his heart warmed up, as he was also more so looking for a mother for his daughter than for a woman to warm his bed.

'Alright,' he told her. 'Do not worry about the girls. I will raise them, and I'll leave neither mine nor yours desolate.'

'Then swear on the Koran,' and after he swore, she said 'Now I swear too,' and put both hands on the holy book, murmured a prayer and left without shaking hands. Before turning at the corner of the haystack, 'wait for me tomorrow,' she called and disappeared into the twilight. The next afternoon, she took her daughter, the few belongings they had, and, without bidding goodbye to anyone, she took the road to the Upper Neighbourhood.

Çaush had been standing at the window all day with his eyes on the street, and when he saw her coming, he went down to open the door.

'Do you have any flour at home?' she asked. 'Yes, I do,' he replied.

'I will make pancakes for our wedding and we will have only two guests, our two daughters.'

'I also have honey,' he said.

'All the better, as I will give you, and you only, all my honey, today and for a lifetime.'

The two little girls became friends eating pancakes with honey and fell asleep embracing each other. Ajnurka placed them both in a bed, and covered them with care, which moved the man, and then got into the bed where he was waiting for her, trembling, but she did not notice this, because she had also started trembling herself. Five daughters and a son were also born, but never, neither they nor the children, when they grew up, singled out the first two girls who filled the hearth with love since the first night, when their parents—trembling slightly—fell into each other's arms on a large bed he had brought from a town of northern Greece, where he had had to work as a servant to reach Gevgelija and where his master would often put his head between his knees and hit him with hot twangs. That is why he died twenty years before his wife, some said. Others thought he died of grief, after he buried his youngest daughter, not even fourteen years of age.

21

Çaush's eldest daughter was married to a boy in their neighbourhood, but whose house was at the very end. There were three or four secluded houses called "the Isaacs", but quite often also "the Jews". It was said that one night many years ago, some strangers knocked on the door of the house on the corner of the Neighbourhood. The owner of the house, Zejbek Zeneli, a man with no children or property, went out to the gate and the moment he opened it, he saw a baby in diapers, left at the doorstep and the silhouettes of a couple leaving through the night and sleet. They called them to stop, but the knockers ran and disappeared into the darkness. He took the baby inside to warm up and untied his diapers. He was a wanderer, and from the writing on the diaper embroidery he realised that the child was of Jewish descent. God knows what calamity befell his parents, forcing them leave him on his doorstep, so that he would be provided with a shelter they could not provide.

Zejbek went to Skopje and asked the Jews there about the writing on the diaper. It's the boy's name, they said, he is called Isaac. He brought him up with that name and never told where that child came from, although he had heard the gossip that he had kidnapped that child from the Sharr Mountain stall. When Isaac grew up, having no land or wealth, he too went into exile, like most of the boys of the village. But as they went to sell *boza*[38] and *salep*[39], crackers and candy, Isaac followed his blood and worked with Jewish craftsmen from Skopje and Thessaloniki and learned to be a jeweller and a craftsman of weapons. When he grew up and had made some money, he longed for the village where he had been raised and returned to Bukojna. No one in the village would have his daughter marry him, so he had to get a wife somewhere in the surrounding villages. Their first child was born dead, but she was not allowed to be buried in

---

[38] thick, slightly fermented millet drink

[39] a drink made from the tubers of orchid and hot milk

the village cemetery, and he buried her near the house, by the roots of an old pear planted some years ago by Zejbek, who was no longer alive. Many years later, Isaac himself was also buried there, although he had been given permission to enter the village cemetery, but he had orally expressed his will to be buried next to his first daughter, and, to this day, the place is called "The Tomb of Isaac". Many years later, one of his grandchildren fell in love with Çaush's daughter. At first, he did not want her to marry him, but Ajnurka persuaded him. When the water is clear, do not stop it, let it flow, she told him. When he brought back the bride for the first time, a week after the wedding, he gave his mother-in-law the small yellow bronze binoculars that my grandmother would use until she died.

The house of the Isaacs was full of strange stuff, because all the boys who were born in that household became masters of iron, made rings, watches, bronze buttons for brides' waistcoats, and fixed broken weapons. Everything new in the village was brought by the men of that family: tin pans, the first hunting weapons, the first rifles, the matchsticks, the mirrors, later the binoculars and a Singer sewing machine, which was still working, and, finally, the gramophone, which they call the "box that does not forget". When the gramophone was made to sing for the first time, Grandma left the room, saying that women could not stay in a room where unknown men had come; she was ashamed to be seen by those singing on the turntable.

But all these inventions of the Jews were woven with life and death. One of the grandsons, who was almost the same age as Çaush's last daughter, would visit my grandparents' house quite often and play with his aunt. One day, as she was chasing him around the house, she entered the small room of the house and put the latch on the door. Open it, or I will kill you, he called and pulled out one of the Jewish shooters he had brought with him. Poor boy did not know that there were live caps in it and jokingly pulled the trigger. The bang deafened his ears and he did not hear the sound of the girl's body slamming to the floor. But after a while, a stream of blood came underneath the door and got down the stairs to the first floor. He fled in terror and would have also killed himself, had they not taken the weapon instantly. Sighing was the only sound Çaush was capable of making those days. 'Both the boy and the girl are the blood of my blood; and I have a share in both life and death,' he would say.

Sorrow would never leave him; he never again joined the dance, even though he was known all over Gora, Zhupa and Opoja as an extraordinary dancer, one of those who could dance Luma's or Brod's dance even on a pie-pan or on a floor table. Only after several years, when one of the many grandchildren he had from the girls grew up and they were celebrating his circumcision with pipes and drums, Xhema the piper from Opoja begged him to dance once again for his grandson's sake. He began the dance, danced and danced so much that even the women of the neighbourhood came to watch him. Master Xhema played the pipes like never before, but all of a sudden the dancer stopped and fell to the ground. They made him lean by Shelgu i Vjetër and then carried him home in their arms. As soon as they put him on his Greek bed, and as soon as his wife put her hand on his forehead, he breathed a sigh of relief, without taking his eyes off her. 'He went to his tomb and left me to deal with all the rest,' Grandmother said, whenever death knocked on their door. And death would not overlook knocking on that household's door…

'I buried two daughters; I know neither the home nor the grave of my son; I buried four granddaughters and three grandsons; the husband of the other granddaughter was sentenced to one hundred and one years in prison; I don't know if my brother in Bosnia is dead or alive, the same for my sister; two of my daughters joined their husbands in Banja Luka and I have not seen them in nine years; I endured all these, but I can't seem to bear the shame that ox of a Donguz made me go through. Wash his wife…that broad sprawled naked, O God, why did you punish me with having to see this too? And what about when that idiot called at me from the room he was in, rub her well, up and down, Ajnurka! Oh God, oh God!'

To me, she seemed to have aged a few years at once. 'Why do people age?' I asked without looking into her eyes. 'Why do you want to learn aging, my dear?' She was silent for a while and looked away. 'A mother ages seven years for every child she buries.'

'What about when her husband dies?'

'The pain of mothers all over the world is the same, but the pain of a wife is different all over.' She was silent again.

I could see her bob her head like a dove, and I felt sorry for her.

'I will go and set that scum on fire,' I told her.

'No, no,' she replied. 'Let's go out on the porch and look through the binoculars. It is a different world when you look at it with the eyes of a Jew…' We looked at the mountains and meadows; Gjallica reached the yard; the forest across seemed to be moving inside the "eyes of the Jew", but when I lowered my binoculars to see the streets and yards of the village, she stopped me.

'Do not look inside the houses, because it is as if you were a thief robbing them.'

On the street, beyond the patio I noticed my paternal uncle, waving and calling to us.

'Come in, what's the matter?' Grandmother shouted.

'I am not coming, no, but my friends sent me to ask you to give us the Koran of your house, as it is the oldest in the village, because we will go to the mountains to distribute the land. We will take the oath on the Koran…'

'Hmm' Grandmother murmured with her eyes on me, but I did not know what to say.

'Do this favour for the highlands,' shouted Uncle from below.

'When are you going?' Grandma asked.

'They have not fixed the date, but they will let us know…'

'Okay, okay, but the Koran will be carried by this grandchild of mine. Otherwise, I won't give it to you.'

'Promise,' Uncle said and returned towards the Lower Neighbourhood. Grandma looked at me proudly. Then, she took the binoculars again to see the world through the eyes of the Jew.

22

Many days passed waiting for Uncle to call me. I had told Mother that I would go to the mountains to hold the Koran, on which the men of both villages would swear, and she looked at me with that boundless human warmth that waved calmly in her eyes and then said: 'You have grown, son!'

When I realised that I was waiting in vain, I went to my uncle's house, which was next to ours. The first person I met was my grandmother who lived with him, as he was her youngest son. In fact, she had another, even younger son, but he had moved to town together with his family, and it was said that he worked in the committee with the balcony.

'Why did you get up so early, as if you're going to be the woodcutter for a wedding?' she asked.

'Isn't Uncle here?' I answered with a question.

I would not stay with my grandmother a lot, because I was afraid of the way she treated us; it often seemed to me that also my father, uncles and aunts were afraid of her, or it was the respect towards a mother's authority, the one who keeps the keys to the house. Everyone answered to her, even when Grandfather was still alive. I didn't remember him, as I was little when he passed away, but I would often look at a big picture of his, which hung on the shelf, and in which he posed with two revolvers in his waist, along one of his sons and his partisan friends, and I wondered how this man with two revolvers had confided the keys of the house to his wife. 'The revolvers were not his,' Grandmother once told me, 'the partisans put them on his waist when they photographed him. Then, they took them back, of course, as they needed them for the war.'

When the boys worked in Durrës as well-known confectioners of the city and had a shop on the boulevard "King Zog", which was later named the boulevard "Count Ciano", he would go every six months, load two horses with flour, sugar, salt, oil, kerosene, soap and Italian pasta, receive a handful of money and come back to the village. But on one of these trips, even before he reached the village, he sent word to his sons to send him money, because he was totally broke. They asked and came to learn what had happened, and from that day on, they sent the money to their mother, whereas he was only given the provisions for six months. On the last trip, Grandfather had stopped at an inn, in the city of Dibra, and some men there had made fun of him, using those gibes Dibra was known for. He took it for as long as he could and eventually he called the innkeeper. 'How much does it cost to have the whole inn for a night?' he asked. The innkeeper, who grasped the issue right away, told him a price twice as high. Grandfather took out his pouch, covered the price the innkeeper asked and also gave him everything that was left in his pouch. 'Now take all these out, for, tonight, the inn is mine.' So he was left without a penny. Moreover, a few days after reaching home, he found out that he had also been left without the keys of the master of the house. I felt sorry for my grandfather, even though I didn't remember anything in relation to him, just the portrait of the man with two revolvers stuck in his belt, in black *tirq*[40] and a white cap on his head, tied with a black dotted handkerchief. He agreed to appear in that photo, only after he was convinced that the partisans that he had welcomed to his house did not steal anything. In the morning, he saw that the four bags of "Tarabosh" tobacco he had left in the room set for them were not touched and told the commissar to take a photo, for which the commissar lent him the two revolvers. 'These partisans of yours are good, Commissar,' he told him. 'They did not touch anything, but they are still in *opingas*. Yet, I don't know what they will do when they start wearing shoes and boots.'

I had heard strange things about their marriage, as well. When my grandmother's father came to learn that he wanted to marry his daughter, while sitting along other men on the *greda*—a large carved trunk leaning on two stones—he said: 'Who, is it him who wants to marry my Raikuna? No, never! Not before filling one hood with gold!' Grandfather, who was a poor orphaned boy and whose four sisters had married far away and could not help him, didn't know what to do. He went on exile for three years, to Thessaloniki, to Janjevo, and even to Romania, but he didn't save up more than eight golden coins. One day, Selman Memisha, a neighbour of our relatives and who, at the time, was one of the richest people in the village, told Grandfather: 'Do not whine, I will go and fill his hood!' One afternoon, together with his friends, he visited

---

[40] Long pants worn traditionally by the men of the region

grandmother's father. They had coffee and pear juice, played cups and, finally, one said: 'Let's not forget why we are here.'

'He knows why we are here,' Selman Memisha said. 'Thank goodness his hood is little…' Still sitting cross-legged, my great-grandfather threw his hood on Selman's lap, while he, quietly, took out two pouches, emptied them into the hood and slid them in front of the former's feet. The two looked at each other's eyes, as if they had come to know each other that evening. Great-grandfather took only eight coins from the hood and returned it to Selman. 'Why don't you take them?' he asked in surprise. 'Because I do not want to marry my daughter off to a house in debt; I took what is mine, you keep what is yours.'

As I waited for Uncle to get out of his room, I wondered if he, too, was afraid of my grandmother. But, after a while, I could bear it no longer, so I asked again and found out that my uncle had left early in the morning. I froze for fear that he had forgotten that I too would go and hold the Koran, on which the men would swear for the highlands.

'We had agreed to go to the mountains…that is, I would go with him,' I whispered.

'What business would you have in the mountains?' Grandmother asked. I didn't answer because I didn't want to tell her anything about the Koran of my other grandmother. I was aware that they—God knows for what reason on earth—had quarrelled years ago and didn't give each other leeway.

Luckily, Uncle's wife, who imitated her mother-in-law in authority and sternness, had just entered the big room and told me that they would not go to the mountains on that day. The villagers with whom we were in dispute over the mountains had come up with some new objections, and it wasn't certain on what day the boundaries would be settled. I felt somehow liberated and began to look at my grandmother more attentively. She pulled out a small key that she had sewn and tied in the pocket of her vest, opened a cupboard—as small as half a window—which was on the wall, and pulled out a candy she handed me. 'She might not be as stern as I thought,' I said to myself. Yet, when she saw that I put the candy in my mouth, in her commanding voice, she told me to get up and help her.

'C'mon, get on this stool, as we'll clean the swallows' nests.'

On the three walls of the room, which was also used to host guests and where there was only an iron bed for Grandmother, there were beautiful brown wooden shelves carved in Prizren, filled with all kinds of dishes, pots, coffee mills, photo frames, an ironing iron not used by anybody, coffee cups from Istanbul or Solun—as my grandmother used to refer to Thessaloniki—and I don't know what else. On the corner over the shelf and the other walls of the room, there were seven swallow nests. In spring, my grandmother would leave the windows open all day and for years no one touched the nests. I got on the chair. 'Not that one,' Grandmother said. 'It's clean as no swallows came there this year.' I started to clean the others, and she watched me attentively. I don't know if it was to check my work, or because she was worried that I could fall off the chair and break any ribs. She herself had suffered from this once—many years ago—when she had fallen while chasing a fly away and had spent several weeks in bed, because of two cracked ribs. But since her room had turned into a salon for swallow nests, the flies were gone.

Waiting for and seeing off the spring birds turned into her life passion. She'd feed them, give them water to drink and, during spring, her room was always full of swallow chirps; they felt at home. As fall approached, she tied threads or thin colourful pieces of cloth on them and the following spring she waited to see if any of them would return. The most favourable spring was the one when four returned.

'How many came back this spring?' I asked. She was pleased that I was curious about an important part of her life and told me that only two had come.

'This winter was fiercer than the last, it weakened both us and the swallows,' she said as if not to blame the birds that hadn't come back. When I finished cleaning all the nests, she opened the shelf on the wall again and gave me a small delight, square in shape and pink in colour. I was so happy, because I had not tasted such a delight for a long time. We used to have some of them, as well. Mother kept them in some coloured tin cans on which the word "Ambrosoli" was written, but they had been missing for years. Even though I had checked inside the boxes several times, they were all empty. 'Tin cans don't birth delights,' Mother had told me.

'Are you cleaning the nests again?' asked my uncle's wife. 'It's the seventh time you clean them,' she added and left the room. Grandmother pursed her lips.

'A house that is not cleaned every day remains dirty no matter what,' she said and began to deal with other work. I started feeling like a burden, and, after losing hope of being given another delight, I left and went down to the centre of the village where Uncle's cafe was.

23

'I'm glad you're here,' Uncle said. He took off his ring and gave it to me. 'Go to Basrije and tell her to give you the big notebook of the events of the village. Bring it to me as soon as you can because these tired people who have come from afar are waiting.'

At a table, I saw two men and a woman, drinking tea and talking in a low voice. You could notice from far away that they were not from our regions.

'Listen, I almost forgot,' Uncle shouted from behind, 'also bring a pickaxe and a shovel.' When my aunt gave me everything I asked for, I inquired about the ring:

'Will you keep it?'

'Of course! This is your uncle's *firman* and nothing in our house can be done without the *firman*.'

When I got back, the three newcomers were out in the cafe yard and were looking at the streets and the houses. In the cafe's front wall, there was a hammer and sickle; the words 'Long life to the strategist comrades' had been written horizontally, whereas the names of Stalin and Enver had been written vertically below. '*Why is this Stalin still there, how can a dead person live long?*' I thought. But I was soon scared of those things that roared in my stupid noggin. 'How's it your problem?' I told myself. We got inside and Uncle took a large notebook out of the leather bag, larger than the ones for school. 'Book of Accounts—Kingdom of Albania' I read on the cover.

Inside the cafe, there was just Olloman America drinking tea and dozing off. Uncle sat on a table with the three newcomers and started flipping through the large notebook. I stood a little to the side for fear of being noticed and sent away: in our village, children were not allowed in cafes. He flipped through the thick notebook and exclaimed:

'I found it. Here it is...your brother was killed on June 23, 1949.'

'Yes, true,' the woman confirmed, 'we came to find out three days later.'

'Look. Or can't you read the handwriting? Today, the news that soldier Servet was killed at the border, in an attempt to escape to Yugoslavia reached the village. Many soldiers have come to the village; they are to be seen in the streets at daytime and not only guarding at night, as before…This is what I wrote at the time. I also noted where he was buried, as they did not place any marks, since he was deemed a traitor to the homeland…But all the evils were brought onto him by that aspirant. He was the filthiest man our village has ever seen. Do you know what he did? Let me tell you a few things…'

Uncle started flipping through the notebook again.

'Look here…March 19, 1949…The officers who came to serve in the village see it beneath them to sleep in the barracks, where the state appointed them. Instead, they force the Council to take them into the houses of the villagers. Many were the men gathered in Adem's cafe today, when, by evening, a soldier came and asked all the councillors of the Front to go to the office. Aspirant Shefqet, who wanted 5 more places for his guests that night, had asked for them. The councillors objected. We can't afford to provide for them every day. The people are poor; they have no food, no bedding and no kerosene for lamps. The aspirant scolded them. Let them drink vinegar, if they have no food! The state has given you the ration and you will look after the state, and the state here is us. The councillors, compelled, appointed two of them at the Tales and the three others at Aliajs…Look, another one…April 15, 1949,' Uncle said, looking through the notebook with a thick cover…In the evening, I went to the mosque, as we had been notified of a meeting. The aspirant will speak, I was told. He came arrogantly and said: 'From now on, the land across the big stream cannot be worked by anybody without my permission! But half of our land is there, someone objected. Live with the other half, the aspirant ordered. Even along the line Druri i Vetmuar[41]—Pyramid Seventeen—from the Plains and up to Kodra e Nikollës[42], nobody is allowed to pass. They are tying us like barges with iron belts throughout the border…'

'Stop yammering,' Olloman said without opening his eyes. 'They are here to deal with their own issues, not our village's.'

'Our issues and theirs are tied together as the rope to the saddle,' Uncle answered. 'Let me also read to you about Ahmet, on June 6, 1949…' Ahmet went to the Locality office. He tied the horse to a meadow to graze until he was

[41] The Lonely Wood
[42] Nikolla's Hill

done. The aspirant passed by, took his horse and rode it back the village. Poor Ahmet, when he did not find his horse, asked around and was told that the aspirant had taken it. 'Have you also become a horse thief now?' he asked the aspirant. 'Don't talk too much or you'll get smacked.' the other replied. Ahmet was so revolted that he went home, talking to the horse that followed him: 'Did you hear? Did you hear me or not? May my five years of suffering and sacrifice in the war be cursed; may my wounds and the blood I shed for the liberation of this country and the pursuit of gangs also be cursed, if a crook of an aspirant can step all over us!'

'Indeed,' said the older man, who was the husband of the killed soldier's sister. 'We were told that brother intended to flee, and he was called a traitor for eight years, but it's now revealed that it was the aspirant who had intended to flee. Servet didn't allow him, and he killed him for fear that Servet would report to the state...'

'Well, let's get going, because it is a long way to the red plum, where your brother was buried,' said Uncle. 'While you,' he turned to me, 'go and take this to my wife.' And he gave me the bag with the big notebook where not only the accounts of the Kingdom but also those of our village were recorded.

24

They went away, and I headed home. Thousands of things crossed my mind, buzzing like angry bees, but there was no power that could keep me from opening that notebook, in which Uncle, just like the poet that Teacher had told me about, noted the secretly killed, whose names and the place where their bones rested were unknown. I didn't know where to hide, but I eventually sheltered myself in the barn near the house. I started reading…The first page was March 11. March 11, 1949…An unknown feeling made my body shiver when I read my uncle's words about me. 'Today,' he had written, my elder brother's son turned three years old. I was asked to cut his hair for the first time. Sister-in-law had prepared *fli*; we ate it with honey and we were all happy, but she was upset…'Will this boy be ok?', she asked. 'He turned three, yet the only thing he has said is "meow…meow"' to the cat, neither father nor mother yet.' *So weird*, I thought, *couldn't I speak?* I kept reading but my mind was there, at the grave of the unknown soldier, who, that day, was turning from traitor to martyr. His brother and his sister, along with her husband, had come from afar. We travelled for three days, they said, from a place I had heard for the first time—its name was Devoll. They'd take his bones and after eight years, they would bury him where his mother and father, his grandfather and great-grandfather rested…I kept reading in fear, in case they had finished early and Uncle caught me with his notebook in hand, which one could only read if they had been given his *firman*. And reading what Uncle had written, one page after the other, added to my fear.

I kept reading until the moment when the lightning of fear burned throughout my body: Uncle is back! I ran and gave the bag to his wife. She thought that I had been with her husband, who had just entered the house. Thus, I fled from the "trial" I could be put through. I ran as if someone was following me; I believed I heard women screaming and dogs barking, dead men wailing and the hungry begging, wolves howling and lambs bleating…I ran and when I collapsed behind a door, I noticed that I was in front of Teacher's room. He was shocked to see me.

'What is it?'

I entered and stood for a few minutes without uttering a word; he gave me a glass of water to drink, put his hand on my shoulder and did not ask further. When I told him everything I had seen, heard and read, he calmly told me:

'Interesting! Your uncle keeps a diary for the village. And who would think that that quarrelsome man kept a diary!'

I was not happy when he called my uncle quarrelsome, but I did not make a sound. As if he had noticed my discontent, he added:

'But he is quarrelsome for the right causes.'

I was pleased with the way Teacher corrected himself, and I somehow came to my senses and asked him what a diary was. When he explained it to me, I remembered the first sentence in Uncle's notebook: Today, on March 11, 1949, I am starting to write about the events of my village...He had been writing without ever growing tired for all these long years. 'A weird man, my uncle! Mows, hoes, goes for wood, walks for nine hours on foot to the city Bazaar, goes to the mill and the cafe and comes back to write in this diary, or whatever they call it...'

'Did you read a lot?' Teacher asked.

'I did not read every page of it, but I reached the point of Stalin's death.'

'Ah, interesting!' he said.

As soon as the thought came to me, I asked him: 'What about your city, does anyone keep a diary there?'

'Who knows,' he said, 'why are you asking?'

'In case someone like Uncle keeps one, they could find the bones of the poet, just as we found the soldier's bones today.'

Teacher did not speak; he stood up and moved in front of the lamp so that his face was not seen. *Maybe he is in tears*, I thought, but I quickly wiped that sudden image from my troubled mind.

I don't know why I put my hand in my pocket but it seemed like I had put it onto an open flame. An envelope, which I had found in Uncle's bag, was still in my pocket. Out of fear and confusion, I had forgotten to place it back where it belonged.

'What is it?' Teacher asked, but I was so confused that I could not even tell him; I only kept looking at the envelope with two foreign stamps, one of which was the portrait of a man, with "Tito" written below. I was terrified. The envelope had been opened. I pulled out the piece of paper and showed it to Teacher.

'Aha,' he said, 'it is an article published in a Zagreb magazine and which talks about your Gora, but about that part of it that is across the border. Where did he get it?'

'A cousin of his there, a certain Majlo; he might have sent it.'

'Could be,' Teacher said, looking through the papers curiously. Then he sat down on the chair and started reading aloud…

'On the border, in the direction of Albania, as a kind of battlement between the two states, in 18 secluded villages of the Sharr Mountains, live the Gorans, who are claimed by four nations and one nationality, but who don't know to whom they belong. They live within the fog and great poverty, as orphans.'

Someone who happens to pass through these villages, on the border with Albania, does not need facts to understand their poverty. It offends the eye at every step and pierces the bone to the marrow. If one asks: 'Who are the Gorani?' he receives an answer that seems to come from the hereafter: 'We are orphans and Gora is distant and desolate.'

25

Interlude

For several days in a row, I went to my grandmother's house every morning, sometimes barefoot and without even washing my face. Every single time she would ask me, why did you get up this early, Grandma's sweetheart, and I would give her the same answer, I am looking for Uncle to go to the mountains. Sometimes, I found them eating trahana[43], but I didn't sit on the table as I was afraid that they would think that I was getting up that early to eat from their trahana. The truth was that it wasn't the mountains that made my mind race, and I worried that my grandmother would grasp this. After a few days of asking the same question about where Uncle was and if he had gone to the mountains, and them giving the very same answer that he was in the cafe, I finally received the answer I had been expecting for so long: Uncle had left for the city to buy goods for the cafe and in case he did not find what he needed, he would also go to Shkodra, because smuggled goods were easier to find there.

I went downstairs and entered an alcove that was still called the photography room ever since the uncle who now lived in the city had placed a camera with which he took pictures. It was said that, again, it was the Jews to have taught him this craft, but not the ones from our village, but the Jews of Vlora, where he had been to school before the war.

With trembling hands, I opened the closet and upon seeing the notebook, I shuddered. It was as if I touched a piece of ice that burned my hands, but I did not give up. I took it and put it under my shirt and left without making a sound. I locked myself in one of the rooms of the house and did not go out at all; I would have stayed even in the evenings—for as long as I could still see—but, as we had no kerosene for the lamp, at night, I crawled on the bed sheets until sunrise.

---

[43] Soup with dried yogurt

Occasionally, I'd leave the room and ask if Uncle was back, and when they told me that he had gone to Shkodra, my shudders of fear would subside. 'I have time,' I would think. After six or seven days, or more—I had no idea how many had passed—I returned the big notebook to its place and took my two notebooks to Teacher. 'Here you are,' I told him, 'I copied my uncle's diary for you.'

'The whole thing?' he asked. 'No, I left out many parts, as I was scared; I wrote the parts that seemed the most beautiful to me…how can I put it…in fact, there was nothing beautiful, but since you told me that this work of my uncle is interesting, I brought it for you.'

'Did anyone see you?' Teacher asked.

'No, nobody at all! My uncle is in Shkodra, the others were having trahana. Thankfully, they did not see me. I was very scared, so I did not copy many of the days,' I said in an apologetic tone.

Teacher put his hand on my shoulder, took the two notebooks I had brought, and sat down to read them. I would put wood to the fire and occasionally look at him; he seemed to not be in the room at all, as if he had immersed himself in the suffering of our village, which my uncle had cut like beech wood and piled up in there, without stacking them.

March 11, 1949

Today I started to write about the events in my village. We call the system democratic. Enver Hoxha is our leader. Six months ago, the border with Yugoslavia was closed. Many villagers and families remained there. So far, we have been friends with Tito. Soldiers have come to the village. We are fed up to the back teeth with drudgery.

So far, the winter has been dry, but there has been a lot of fog. Ten days ago, there was up to a meter of snowfall. Grass is sold at 6–10 lek per kilo. The state supplies us with grain, 10 kg per capita. We were supplied until March 30; nobody knows what we will do afterwards. Our minds are in the fog! The state sells the grain to us for 4–5 lek per kilo. The cost of bringing it from Kukes is 1 lek per 5 kilos. In the free market, grain is sold for 40–50 lek / kg, but it is not easily found. From families that breed over 10 heads of livestock, the state requires 1 kilogram of meat per head; the meat is paid 22–25 lek per kilo. Today we learned that soldiers have arrived in the villages of Pakisht, Zapod, Bele and Kosharisht; the border is being fortified. In the evening, the council assigned two officers to Hamza, who asked for a good room with plenty of light, claiming that they had important work to do at night.

March 12, 1949

A few days ago, some men from the village were called to arms. A marketplace is nowhere to be found. It has been three months since we received the food ration. Soap is not to be found even to wash the dead. The soldiers stationed in the village killed Shaqir from Cërneleva, near the border; nobody knows why. The soldiers do not allow us to work the land located less than 500 m near the border; this also depends on the post commander's mood.

March 20, 1949

A big storm started; the corners of the houses are filled with snow, the gale is scratching the walls. Murk and fog. In the morning, in the cafe, people said that Sabir covertly checked the houses to learn who has grain and where they took it from and reported to the security guards. As we talked, Sabir unexpectedly came and learned the accusation of his fellow villagers. Embarrassed, he said that he is not the only one doing this job and told us the others' names. So many spies in the village. We were speechless when he said: 'We are striving for the good of the people.'

March 23 1949

The fog did not clear up all day long. The chairman of the committee in Bicaj came to the village; he stayed for a while in the council office and left for the Locality. We don't know why he came.

I learned that the state sells 1kg of coffee for 1000 lek and 1kg of sugar for 350 lek; this is not for the people, only for the cafes. Thank God, there are no cafes left in the village. At night, I hosted three officers, while two others stayed at Sallah's house.

March 28, 1949

Some from the Locality came to the old grove and cut firewood, accompanied by soldiers. Our councillors complained about this to the aspirant. He replied, 'I was the one to grant them permission.' Both commander of the border and owner of the village!

March 28, 1949

Downpour! It snows and hails. Today I was in the Locality and there I learned that Enver Hoxha, along with seven others, went to Russia. It's not clear why they went. Xheladin came from Kukës and says: 'Great poverty, very high prices, there is nothing in the market.'

April 3, 1949

The village learned that the ration lists have arrived; according to them, state employees and families whose men are in the military service will be given 8 kilograms of grain per capita. While the poor, orphans and the disabled only 4 kg per capita per month. Families that have more than two sheep per capita are not given any supplies; they are considered wealthy ranchers. And when they complain, they are told: Give meat, and we give you grain. Indisputable offer, 1 kilogram of meat for 22 lek. They take our meat five times cheaper than the price of cottage cheese in the marketplace!

April 21, 1949

I was ploughing and for the first time I heard the cuckoo. I lifted the biggest stone I found nearby, I put it over my head and threw it behind my back. It is customary, so that the butter in the churn is abundant.

May 2, 1949

On Monday, the sister of my sister-in-law Refija passed away. May she rest in peace! She left behind a married son and a married daughter, two bachelor sons and three unbetrothed daughters. She was bedridden for six long months.

They are starving! Today, I planted corn behind the house. I'm afraid this year's fog will ruin the blossoms of trees.

May 4, 1949

The traditional feast of Saint George began today. The children got up early in the morning, went to collect flowers with which they will bathe for Saint George's.

May 5, 1949

The rites of Saint George's continue: today is the day of cutting willows, which symbolises renewal; they are placed on the doors of houses, in fields and meadows. Lovers compete to find the largest and most robust willow to place on the gate of their beloved. Brides and girls go to collect herbs and plant roots to give to the cattle in order to encourage more abundant milk. The joy and happiness of the holiday is not as it used to be. People are hungry; our rations are not given regularly. There is no grain in the market and, in case you find it, you have to pay 150 lek per kilogram.

May 6, 1949

On Saint George's Day, we did not go out to Uranok because we had no coffee and sugar. Today is Friday; the elders say it is not good luck for Saint George's to fall on a Friday.

May 10, 1949

Foggy weather, not a single drop of rain for days: crops have not yet covered the ground. The elections for the village council will be held, 5 candidacies have been submitted: Abdyl, Nebi, Qamil, Adem, Omer. The first three are red, while the last two are white. It is clear who is going to win.

June 1, 1949

Together with three or four fellow villagers, I left for Peshkopi. On the first day, we travelled to Shumbat, we spent the night there and the following day, we parted. Rahman and I continued our way to Peshkopi, Qemal and Harun set off towards the villages of the area to look for grain. Rahman and I, passing through the village of Suhadoll, stopped at a house to ask for bread. An old woman came to the door. After giving us bread, she asked: 'Have you not brought any alltan (golden coin) to exchange for grain?'

'Yes,' we said, 'how much grain will you give us in return?' She replied bluntly: 70 kilograms of corn. We continued our way to the bazaar of Peshkopi. The bazaar was full of people and goods. A horse was sold for 60,000 lek, a cow for 35,000. After walking around the bazaar and getting what we needed, we returned to Suhadoll, where we got 70 kilos of corn for a golden coin. We set off for Kala e Dodës[44], where we spent the night.

June 4, 1949

Nothing special. People have gone to the Locality. They were summoned for a meeting as someone from Tirana had come; in the evening, they returned from the meeting, where they heard the speech of the envoy from the centre, sent to communicate the new decision of the Government on the obligations that farmers must abide by. Specifically, from now on, the Government requires: 15 kilograms of grain per acre, 3 kilograms of meat per acre and 4 eggs per acre. Our poor chickens!

June 9, 1949

Today is a holy night and the voting day. The Lord of heaven and the Lord of the earth have blended. 350 votes were cast for the front (in the full box), 11 votes against (in the empty box). I cast mine against. The entirety of the village would have voted against, but they are scared of the spies, because whoever votes against is considered an enemy of the people and denied the right to a ration.

---

[44] Castle of Doda

June 28, 1949

Murteza from the Locality came to the village to force the people to hand over the meat and grain. His tongue does not rest: 'Whoever does not hand over the obligations, let him leave the village!' And go where?

July 1, 1949

The entire village has left for the Locality, to deliver the meat that the state obliges us to. About 150 cattle were delivered by Bukojna. I have been asked to give 97.4 kg of meat. Today, I handed over 25 kilograms of meat, which I bought at 194 lek / kilogram and handed it over to the state at the price of 8 lek / kilogram. I did not receive this money. I donated it to the Red Cross. Better generous than ripped off.

July 22, 1949

12 people came to the village. They call themselves "the Cultural Brigade". They are convincing us on the benefits that the communists have brought. Unstable weather: sometimes clear, sometimes overcast; the fog licks the roofs of houses.

August 26, 1949

I left to grind in our mill. When I arrived in Gërgojec, I saw Munish from Glloboçica, who was made to march in front of two soldiers. I addressed him: Hey Mesho! And he replied. Then I asked the soldiers: is it allowed to talk to this man and ask him about my aunt who I have not seen for a year and a half? After they gave me permission, I asked him about all our relatives and acquaintances the border separated us from. He told me they are in good health.

October 21, 1949

Albanian soldiers killed Bajram from Shishtavec. He had gone to the mountains to mow the grass. They, thinking that he was fleeing, shot him without warning and left him dead.

December 8, 1949

The plenipotentiary of the obligations came from Kukës. He gave us an ultimatum to pay all the obligations within 7 days by delivering them to the Locality. People are very stressed. Those coming from Kukës say that soldiers have settled in Zminec and ask for a permission pass to go from Gora to Kukës. O great God, have they set yet another border for us?

December 31, 1949

Since it is the last night of the year, Omer, Bajram, Dallfit, Rexhep, Sabir and I gathered in "Monte Carlo", as we call Sabir's house, where we often gamble at night. We played thirty-one to try our luck. The game continued until dawn. Dallfit and I won two kilos of potatoes each.

January 12, 1950

Two envoys have come to the village to demand the obligations. They do not care whether we have them or not. Now the ration is given solely to 35 families; they are given 3 kilograms per capita per month.

January 18, 1950

People continue to deliver their obligations to the Locality. Rainy weather and a wind blowing from the south. There has been no snowfall yet, but there is a lot of fog, murky and cold. Tomorrow Ramiza will marry Uko from Oreshka. No one in our village married her, as Kluce "removed her headscarf", but she refused to become his wife.

January 19, 1950

In the morning, I went to open the cafe as usual. From the window, I saw the Oreshkas who took poor Ramiza as if she were a widow. O Kluce, what have you done to this girl! A lump was stuck in my throat.

January 22, 1950

In the evening, two "black policemen" came. (The police officer of the Locality who serves with a short rifle and civilian clothes is called a 'white policeman', while those with uniforms, German rifles and holsters are called 'black policemen'). We saw them while in the cafe. They went straight to Ismail Kasem's house, to search it. During the search, they found 18,000 dinars earned with hard labour in Bihac of Bosnia. They took the money and went to search Ali Kalizi's house. They also found a lot of dinars there and took them as well. Finally, they went to the Huliq family in Mumin Hoxha's house. What they found there is not known yet. It could be learned tomorrow. During the raid, all their belongings—clean and dirty—were turned inside out to find whatever they were looking for.

January 25, 1950

The bonds for the rations are here. We will be provided with 5–6 kg of grain per capita. People went to the Locality to get their rations, but not all of them were given it. Tobacco papers have not been available for over a month and villagers smoke tobacco wrapped in newspaper.

February 24, 1950

We left for Kukës before dawn and reached the town in the afternoon. Tefik arrived later and told us that Halil Tuçe together with four others had fled to Yugoslavia: he and his wife, their 7-year-old son and two little daughters. Those who know his suffering well say that he fled to escape hunger; he had no food to eat.

April 30, 1950

Dry foggy weather. The crier announces: All the families who are obliged to deliver meat will take the cattle to the mosque tomorrow and from there they will be sent to Kukës. Most people don't have anything to deliver; some are asked for too much. It is calculated based on the surface of land. Thus, Father Stalin commanded: meat and wool for every acre! One could own land, but if he owns no livestock, where is he supposed to find the meat?

May 23, 1950

The news spread that the police had injured and captured Zaim Banushi from Kollovoz alive. Two years ago, the police had taken the man from his house, but on the way, he had fled. Afterwards, he remained a runaway in the mountains for a long time. He eventually surrendered himself to the police. After the split from Yugoslavia, he escaped from prison and crossed the border. Now they have caught him again.

July 12, 1950

All villagers who own meadows in Senakofce went to mow them. After mowing the meadows left to them by their fathers and grandfathers, they have to deliver half of the grass to the border post for free and only keep the remaining half for themselves. In the Ottoman period, the state received "one tenth". These demand half!

July 27, 1950

I went to the graves of Gushaja to collect and transport grass. As soon as I arrived, in front of me, just across the border, two Serbian soldiers brought to the border a mare followed by its pony. I approached to see them. When I reached the fields of Roçkë, a man from Glloboçica was standing beyond the border. As soon as he saw me, he went down to the stream and got closer to me. Then I was heartened and asked, 'Is Aunt Hiba alive?'

'Yes,' he replied. 'Who are you?'

'I am her nephew. Say hello to her from me!'

'I will,' he told me, and we parted as if in a dream. The soldiers did not see us. Or they did not want to.

August 16, 1950

Two black policemen and a Locality policeman came to raid some houses to take their grain, as they had not paid off their obligations for 1949. But it was in vain; you can't find clothes on the naked!

December 21, 1950

Our state is celebrating Stalin's birthday. On this occasion, we also organised a dinner for the villagers in my cafe. 30 people gathered and we prepaid 60 lek per person. We cooked meat, beans and halva, which, in our tradition, is the menu of the death ceremony. Nobody got the trick.

January 18, 1951

Today is the day of water (Vodice). Boys and girls, but also men and women wet each other with water and exchange jokes. The main street of the village is bustling with life. After dinner, we played the spoons on the windows of the houses. People believe that spraying water on this day brings good luck, while knocking spoons scares the vampire off or, as they call it in our village, "Azhderhana".

January 21, 1951

Monday. In our village, the first sheep has given birth. The lamb is a white male. Three and a half months to Saint George's. Clear and very cold weather.

February 1, 1951

I learned that two women in our neighbourhood quarrelled: one had many children and the other none. The first spoke to the cattle she was taking to drink water: 'Look, look at our household, the goats fertile, the sheep fertile, the cows fertile and the women fertile.' The other took these words personally, and they grabbed each other by the hair and exchanged offenses that cannot be written.

March 18, 1951

I left for Kukës. I reached the city in the afternoon. There, it was said that Zaim Banushi from Kollovoz was executed on the bank of Drini i Zi[45], near the bridge, and was left there to be seen by the people. I went to see him. And see what?

March 29, 1951

Ismail's wife went to pyramid 17, to see if they would return the horse that had crossed the border yesterday. She also took her two daughters. After waiting for a while, they started singing in Gorani:
'Haj mori, shto me sllushate,
Dali mi kona vidohte?'
Three women that were collecting kindling on the other side of the border also replied singing:
'Ne trazhi kona v'shumishta,
Trazhigo ka ke Vranishta,
Tamo go zeha askeri,
Askeri, xhidi laskeri.'
The guards who were in the barracks heard them, but did not understand the words of the song. Suspicious, they asked a shepherd: What do those singing say? He translated the words for them: her horse is lost and she asked them if they had seen it, and the three women across the border told her that the horse had been taken by the Yugoslav soldiers to Vranisht.
Ismail's wife was escorted to the Locality, where she was interrogated, but later they let her go. In the evening, two black policemen came to the village and at three o'clock after dinner they took her to the Locality again. The council did not leave the matter in the hands of the two police officers, but appointed Dallfit to accompany them. Nothing to be done; here at the border, one could lose his horse, and even his wife!

---

[45] Black Drin

April 2, 1951

In the evening, the crier announced: 'All villagers, men and women, with the right to vote, are to gather at the mosque. The council chairman, who has not worked in the benefit of the village, will be dismissed.' After discharging him on the spot, another one was elected to temporarily substitute him.

April 21, 1951

Harun Tada brought a rooster to my shop to sell. We asked him to sell it to us for 120 lek, and then put in a trade lottery; 15 people gave 10 lek each and, thus, 150 lek was collected; we bought it for 30 more lek than the first offer. In the trade lottery, the rooster was won by Abdyl. Lucky man; three weeks ago, he was dismissed from the position of the council chairman and today he won the rooster!

April 25, 1951

The bailiff came from Kukës, he seized Haki's donkey in exchange of the 3700 lek he owes to the state for the court expenses. The donkey's gone for seven movie tickets which he wanted to smuggle.

May 20, 1951

In the village of Kosharisht, we met some people who came from the city, they told us that Vuke from our village was arrested, as he and his friend, with whom he worked in the grain warehouse, manipulated the weight and stole from the rations! His friend, a man from Prizren, had not waited for the police to come, he had gone to the bridge over Drini i Zi and ended his life by jumping into the river.

June 5, 1951

The first day of Ramadan. People are hungry; most are fed on herbage only. Grain is sold 100–135 lek per kilogram, but is not to be found. The women go every day to the villages that have land under water to find some grain in exchange for clothes and jewellery. Brides do not spare even their bridal clothes to save their children from starvation!

July 12, 1951

Today, we went to the border again to collect the grass, each from their own property. I took my mother and wife with me. When we got there, we saw that Aunt Hiba from Glloboçica had come to see us. She had brought us the socks, a gift from Raif's bride, who got married after the border was closed. Not allowed to hand them over to us, she threw them in a bush across the border, and we took them. Thank God nobody saw that; had someone noticed, we would be damned.

September 29, 1951

Tefik sent away his wife and mother-in-law who had been living with him for 5 years. It is said that he suspected they cast a spell on him. As proof, he had found tufts of goat hair in the mattress.

January 30 1952

All the families of the Upper Neighbourhood went to the Locality to get food with handbills. We were given 50 grams of salt per capita, 600 grams of sugar per capita. Families with children under the age of 7 were also given 600 grams of sugar per family. In the evening, we returned to the village. They immediately called us to a meeting. They are looking for workers for the textile factory which is being built in Tirana.

March 21, 1952

I have been restless these three-four days. A few days ago, Terxia came from the Locality and told me: 'Today, when I was in the Locality, I was summoned by the police and questioned about you: what it is that you do, do you sell yarn, paint, cotton or other goods.' My blood boiled and my vision blurred, and I immediately went home. They want to spy on me; Terxia didn't consent, but it's not difficult to find others; there are many wilful for such work.

April 7, 1952

Two officers came and asked for shelter. We assigned them to Mumin. The Pole of the village accompanied them to the house. After a while, they came to my house: 'Come out, we won't be sleeping in dump!' I replied from my window: 'I don't go out at night.' They said to me, 'Well, you'll see.' Afterwards, they called Sali, also a council member. He went out and asked, 'What's going on; why are you shouting at night?'

'We won't sleep where you assigned us,' they shouted. 'If you don't like the place we assigned you, go and sleep in the barracks,' Sali said, and they went to sleep in the barracks.

May 6, 1952

Today is Saint George's day. Early in the morning, we went to the Upper Hill, to Uranok. There are 99 reasons as to why we are not brewing coffee, as it is customary of the day. First, we have no coffee. Second, we have no sugar.

May 8, 1952

In the morning, all the children and the youngsters of the village passed through the main road, in a sort of procession, holding wet rags on sticks, crying with tears and shouting: 'Holji dadojli, oh God give us some drops of rain, so that we may grow the new grain.' In the evening, we gathered in the mosque to pray to God for rain. The prayer for this occasion was sung by Mullah Rexhep, while we said 'ameen' with our hands open. I wonder, will God hear us?

September 8, 1952

Together with my son and my brother's son, I left for Kukës to hand over the due grain for the mill. Commander Enver is visiting Kukës.

Along with the escort that accompanied him, he arrived in Kukës at 5:30, in European style clothes. People greeted him lined up on both sides of the road, from the bridge over Drini i Zi, to the executive committee or the committee with a balcony, as they call it. As soon as he crossed the bridge, he got out of the car and continued on foot. He proudly waved his hand and met the people who had come out to greet him. People applauded and shouted: 'Long live Enver Hoxha!' He didn't overlook me, either. He was a handsome and confident man. He was followed by officers, their heads also held high. He entered the committee, and, after a while, he went out on the balcony and waved at us with both hands.

November 27, 1952

The school year started 4 months ago. I told my daughter, 'Let's see if you have learned anything.' She had learned nothing. I beat her so severely that blood came out of her nose. But I regretted it; the children are not to blame. The two teachers we have, who receive 5000 lek per month and gamble all day in the cafe, are to blame. They have even started drinking raki[46].

January 6, 1953

Last night, after dinner, at around 10 p.m., I had lost sleep, when the ground started shaking. I got up to look out the window. Everything was white with snow. So far, the weather has been mild.

March 6, 1953

Today, news broke that Stalin—the leader of the Soviet Union and leader of all communist parties in the world—had died. The communists are in mourning, as he was the one to lead them on the path to communism! Shortly after, we learned that Malenkov had taken Stalin's place.

May 20, 1953

Nesibe, Mumin's mother, died today. There was no congregation to bury her, only four people took her to the grave. The men have left the village in search of bread crumbs.

---

[46] A traditional alcoholic drink

July 11, 1953

The riflemen of the village have begun mowing the meadows on the border belt. They made arrangements with the aspirant to mow the meadows of the poor and share half of the grass with the army. This is robbery! But people dare not speak.

October 16, 1953

Three months ago, Hysen divorced his wife, Ramize. But he did not give her anything from her personal belongings. She sued him and was given the right to take her clothes and sleepwear. Today, she took it all.

November 10, 1953

I went to Kukës; there I learned that Ibrahim was found with 12 light bulbs, for which he was prosecuted. Afterwards, Ibrahim sent Vejsel a letter to give to Rahman, so that the latter hid the goods he had sent home. Vejsel had a child deliver the letter to Rahman. At that moment, Rahman's house was being searched by the police and they seized the letter along with the goods Ibrahim had sent from Kukës. They loaded them on Rahman's back and took him to the Locality. The next day, they sent him to Kukës with the load still on his back. While returning from the city, I saw him in Bele.

December 31, 1953

When I returned from Kukës to the village, without thinking twice, I told the ones in the cafe that, in Kukës, it was said that Albania and Yugoslavia had established diplomatic relations. People, whose children, parents and relatives live as expats in Yugoslavia, have spread the rumour that the border will be opened.

At lunch, I came home to grab a bite. Just then, I heard a boy calling to me: 'You have been summoned to the Locality, urgently.' What should I do? It's 9 p.m. I left worried: why are they summoning me this hastily? When I arrived, they asked: Who spread the news that the border with Yugoslavia will be opened? I replied that I didn't say these words, but only said that Albania and

Yugoslavia have re-established diplomatic relations. Just that. The others had spun my words to their liking. I know who ratted on me.

March 1, 1954

1 kilogram of cotton, 1 kilogram of sugar and 6 bars of soap were stolen from the village shop. The Border Post has a dog that tracks wrongdoers. They brought the dog, released him at the cafe and he went to the house of the Damats. They denied having touched what's not theirs. Then, they gathered all the young people in the reading room, and let go of the dog; it went to Shosha and began to growl. Shosha was escorted to the border post prison. In order to carry on with the investigation, the police from the Locality came. Nobody confessed to having been the author of the theft.

During the night, Shosha, Iliaz's wife along with her son and daughter will be kept at the post office; they'll be monitored by a police lieutenant and two police officers.

After dinner we, the councillors, went too; the lieutenant began to tell us about his authority. 'I have the right to arrest; I have the right to beat the suspects,' and many more words that befit a bandit. Eventually, we ran out of patience and retaliated. Kasem said: 'Comrade Lieutenant, with three more bandit officers like yourself, people will die of fear.'

May 30, 1954

Today, we voted for our representative at the People's Assembly. Abdyl Hasani from Nimça, a distinguished shepherd, was elected.

October 2, 1954

Ten families left the village this year.

Everybody is leaving because of the scarcity of food. In order to take the mouth to food, the village is being abandoned.

January 6, 1955

The girls were at a wedding in the Kërpaçës. Vezire, Çapçe's daughter, was also there. Xanxo Bislimi asked two soldiers to help him kidnap the girl. Xanxo had been married, but, at the time he was in the military, his wife ran away, and now he is trying to get married with the help of the military.

January 9, 1955

I am recording the current prices of some agricultural products: Grains for bread are sold from 35–45 lek per kilogram; fodder and oat 20–25 lek / kilogram; Novoseja[47] people sell their potatoes at 8–9 lek per kilogram or we exchange 1 kilogram of cabbage for 2 kilograms of potatoes. Their village produces only potatoes.

January 22, 1955

In the morning, Nuredin's bride came from Shishtavec. On a sorrel horse, and with no bridal veil. She did have an umbrella, as it was raining. She was accompanied only by her younger brother and Hajredin; there was one else to escort her, because her father is a kulak.

August 23, 1955

A man nicknamed Cuckajno—as he sniffles every two seconds—has come to work as a shoemaker in the village. They gave him a gun. He spends all his time with the soldiers and gossips about the village. At night, he goes out with them as a guide, to follow the boys who go to meet their beloved ones. He did not learn his lesson even after the beating he received from Nehat and Sula.

August 27, 1955

As soon as I opened the shop, I heard cries: Berisha has kidnapped Lemsha, Terzia's daughter. He has taken her to Olloman's house, to his uncles. After

---

[47] A village in Kukës, famous for its potatoes

taking her inside, he closed the front door, but she ran out of the window and left him empty-handed.

September 2, 1955

An envoy from the district's finance department came to auction off the items seized from Ibrahim Çuça, who fled to Yugoslavia. The land he owned was given to crowded families who own no land.

October 10, 1955

Political relations with Yugoslavia are considerably less tense. It is rumoured that the borders will be opened. In our village, the lands, forests and pastures will be used as they have been before: everyone on the property they own across the border. So they say...O God, unite what politics has separated!

December 27, 1955

In the evening, through the darkness, the border soldiers, accompanied by some councillors, went to the house of Majlo's wife to expel her along with her 9-year-old son. Her husband, Majlo, works in Zagreb. It is rumoured that she will be sent to some place in Central Albania. She put her personal and sleeping clothes in sacks and loaded them on her horse. They were not allowed to spend the night with their relatives. They spent the night in the border post.

January 11, 1956

Sherif is sitting in the cafe reading the diary of Mullah Isuf, in Turkish; it was started 45 years ago and makes word of all the good and bad events that happened in the village and the province. In one of the pages, we found the depiction of the border between the villages of Borje and Glloboçicë, from Orçusha to Shishtavec, made by the International Borders Commission. They had cut through Gora with an axe!

January 16, 1956

In the morning, as soon as I opened the cafe, the security service lieutenant, Hamdi, came and asked me: 'Did Omer Rahmani speak against the state, after he returned from Yugoslavia, which he was legally visiting?' I said, 'I know nothing.'

'You do know, but you will not tell us,' he replied.

January 18, 1956

The centre has given instructions for the collectivisation of the village. Agricultural cooperatives must be established in every village. So far, 6 agricultural cooperatives have been established in the district of Kukës. During 1956, only the agricultural cooperative of Orgjost was established in the region of Gora. 4 days ago, a cooperative of 18 families was also set up in Shishtavec. People oppose the establishment of cooperatives, as those who do not have people for labour are at a loss; it's better for those families who do.

January 31, 1956

Today is the beginning of the three holy months. Good weather. No animal was sacrificed in the mosque. A man from Oreshka brought a buck to sell. He had previously set the price of 150 lek per kilogram. It is very expensive, so he could not find a customer and took the buck home. In the store, I sold only one kilogram of butter; people have no money.

February 28, 1956

We got up in the morning to a snowstorm. Snow sticks to walls like high-quality plaster. Five fellow villagers on horses are in Kukës to get cement for the fountain. In the evening, the crier announced that all the men of the village should go to accompany them back. From the whole village, only eight people stepped forth. May God spare us; what has become of us!

May 9, 1956

In the morning, news spread of a saboteur from Yugoslavia who had fallen into the ambush of the border guards at the fountain, at the entrance of Pakisht. There, he had killed a soldier and managed to escape. Hence, the alarm was raised, and all forces as well as armed civilians were organised in his pursuit. The gunmen caught him alive, while crossing the Orgjost River.

June 27, 1956

Today, the weather changed. It rained along with a strong wind; it was very cold and, then, snow and hail started. The goats that went out in the morning to graze did not return in the evening; they were trapped by the cold in Dobrajca, in the valleys of Imer. The entire village went to look for them; I found my three goats alive, while over 20 heads had burst from the cold. The shepherd was going mad with grief. What could the poor man do in these times, when it snows even in June!

August, 21, 1956

Tosun, the police lieutenant, together with a policeman, came to the village and raided the houses of Omer and Harun. The first time they searched Omer, they took 40 golden 20 frank Napoleons which belonged to Majlo's wife. Now, when they searched him, they found 5 golden 100 frank Napoleons, ten golden Turkish liras and two golden 20 frank Napoleons which had been buried. It seems that Omer was roughed up in the typical 'security fashion' and was forced to show where he had hidden them—that is, under the doorstep.

September 18, 1956

This year, the sheep of Oreshka, Zapod, Kosharisht and our village will be inseminated at the Artificial Breeding Station. To change the breed of our Sharr Mountain sheep that we have had for hundreds of years, the state has brought a ram of the merinos breed from Mongolia. The station has been established in the house of Kushka and it is operated by Xhevat, who has completed a quarterly course in Tirana...Oh God, protect our women!

Part Two

26

When I got out in the morning, I saw Uncle's horse prepared for travel. Afraid, I ran and asked: 'You aren't leaving for the mountains without telling me, are you?'

'They are going to the Locality, can't you see the policeman waiting for them?' his wife told me, anguished.

'Trouble seems to follow us with this man,' she muttered and went inside. I followed her, and when I entered the room, I saw Uncle having his porridge in sage tea; a habit of his since when was in the army.

'Don't, mother's sweetheart, do not pick on the state!' Grandmother told him.

'If it defends thieves, I don't need the state at all. For what else could it be of any use? To plough my field? I plough it myself. To mow my meadow? I mow it myself. To betroth my son? I betroth him myself. To watch my cows? I watch them myself.'

As he said these words, he had the last spoonful of porridge and got up to leave.

'Don't you think that the state is Abdulka!' Grandmother said, but I am not sure whether he heard those words or not, as he was closing the door behind himself. The sound of the wooden stairs, creaking under Uncle's heavy step, was heard and then a spine-chilling silence. Grandmother got up and went to the window to see off her son going to the Locality, because he was summoned by the police, who were waiting for him a little further, at the fountain. I wanted to learn the reason, but I was afraid that those words that I had heard so many times would be told to me again: 'Why do you poke your nose into others' affairs?' I had no other choice but to ponder on what had happened with Abdulka, who my grandmother just mentioned, a few weeks ago. She was a stout trouble maker living in solitude; no one knew where her husband and sons were, or whether she had any sons at all. It was known that she had married a daughter off to the neighbouring village. I always had a shadow of doubt about those betrothed outside our village. 'Why was Ajsha married off in Shishtavec?'

'They saw her with a soldier beneath the window.'

'Why did Mersije leave for Orgjost?'

'Her husband beat her and she didn't want to even lay her eyes upon the men of our village anymore.'

'Why did Mirzani marry a girl from Novoseja?'

'It is his second wife and only a kulak's daughter would marry a widowed man, as the unmarried are scared of becoming a kulak's son-in-law.' Things like this I also thought of Abdulka, who had no relatives in our village.

Those days, a neighbouring family had complained that the only lamb they owned and kept for Saint George's was lost. Their little daughter said that the lamb had entered Abdulka's house and never left. The following day, Abdulka's daughter, who had come to visit her mother and was on her way back to her husband's house in the other village, had been stopped by the lady whose lamb was lost. 'A pair of socks of mine is lost; someone took them from the fence, I want to check what you have in your bag.' Convinced that she had no socks, she opened the bags. There was a lamb leg in each, but the neighbour made no sound. 'May you eat it for a death ceremony!' she cursed silently and ran to my uncle. 'We have elected you to the council; protect us from the thieves.' He had no choice, so he went to Abdulka. 'I have to search, because a lamb has gone missing,' he told her. 'Sit down, and let me bring you a glass of buttermilk.' She went out and returned with the buttermilk jug. Uncle looked at her with suspicion, not only because it took her a little long to be back but also because he noticed something under her clothes, which made Abdulka look even fatter. 'What are you hiding in your chest?' he asked. 'Have you come to look for the lamb or for my tits, as I am a woman with no husband and sons at home?' she attacked him and Uncle was intimidated. '*This thief will give me a bad name!*' he thought, confused. 'Okay, let's go out, since you are afraid that I have come to search your tits!' he told her. When they went out, he locked the door. 'I will go and inform all the council members and we will search it,' he said and left without paying any mind to Abdulka's complaints and slanders.

The council members also took a woman along, and when she looked inside Abdulka's clothes, she found a lamb leg. 'Oh, you were not satisfied with one lamb only!' Uncle shouted. They searched her house and found three skins peeled miserably. She began to cry and beg. 'Please, do not take me to the Locality; my daughter's children had no food to eat.'

'If you had told us, the Council would have given you food,' one of the councillors told her. All of them spoke harshly to her, but they eventually let her go and when a councillor proposed to take her in front of the people, they answered: 'Leave the damned thing be, or she may end up hanging herself someplace!' They all agreed, as they were bitterly reminded of Lemsija, a young bride from our village who, when she left and got married in the city, she started work in the confectionery factory. One day, when a search was undertaken, they found a chunk of butter inside her panties. All the workers were gathered to denounce the crime. The chief director and even someone from the committee without a balcony came, and the meeting began. 'Where is she?' the man from the committee asked; everyone turned their heads and looked around, but only Lemsija was missing in that meeting. She was found hanging from the toilet cistern chain. 'The partisan was avenged!' were the words of many people in the village, and they were not opposed even by those who had been against the partisans and had spied on them as much as they had been able to.

I was born a few years after the war, but what people recalled from that time had cemented that event for me and every time I heard it being mentioned, I opened my ears as if it was the stars in the sky whispering. The partisan had come to our village on a winter day; he was together with two others, wounded in an exchange with the forces of the Bajraktar at Kroi i Bardhë[48]. Because of the snow and storm that night, they had crossed the Kollovoz Mountain with difficulty and had come down to our village. They lacked the strength to walk even a step further and knocked on the door of the first house they saw, but unfortunately, it happened to be unwelcoming. The master of the house came out and shouted: 'I don't accept anyone inside, go and stay at the herbage!' He left them outside in the frost. The partisans were about to freeze, the eyes of one of the wounded were about to close and they kept wetting his face with snow, so that he did not fall into the sleep of death. So, the leader of the partisans could not stand it anymore, pushed the door with his shoulders and opened it. 'You are entering by force. You are violating my house!' the villager, a small man, cried. 'Is this how you will make Albania prosper?'

'You are letting us die out in the snow. Two of us are wounded. Do you have Albanian blood or not?' the commander of the partisans replied. 'I have no fire

---

[48] The White Spring

for you!' But the partisan went out, picked up some sticks and twigs from the garden fence and lit a fire. He put a pot on it to scald the clothes and asked for some soap, or a handful of flour if there was no soap, just enough to remove the bad odour from the clothes. 'I'll give you nothing, not even tar; I won't let my bread mix with your lice!' the villager said. At that moment, the room spun from the smack the partisan gave him. That's the whole story, but, the following day, the other Brigade partisans, who came, set up a trial and condemned their comrade. He was shot next to a wild pear tree on the outskirts of the village. It is said that from that day forth, the tree trunk had no more sap under its bark and withered. The house trunk of the peasant who ignited this woe also withered; five years after the war, he was declared *kulak*. Three hundred sheep, three containers with butter and cottage cheese, two crates with honey, all the grain in his barn, and some gold coins, which they found under the threshold of the house door, were taken away. He left the village altogether and married Lemsija off to a town storekeeper. He was later said to have fled again to Patos or Roskovec, where he looked after his family by selling candies and crisps to school children. That's how it went, from unwelcoming to unfortunate.

27

After pondering over these, my mind started roaming aimlessly. I looked at both my grandmother and my uncle's wife and, upon realising that neither was going to tell me why Uncle was being taken to the Locality, I got up and left without making a sound.

For a long time I did not know where to go and whom to ask. At first, I first thought of going to Belçuk or the "King's Boy", as we called him, but I changed my mind right away. 'He is still stuck in the monarchy era, and it never occurs to him to inquire about the village affairs!'

He had been given that nickname since birth, because his parents, slightly slow-witted, were the only ones in the province who agreed to marry, at the king's expense, on the day he got married to Geraldine of Hungary.

Yet, seemingly, my feet had brought me close to our houses, which had been occupied by the soldiers several months ago, upon what we had been scattered like ravens to four other houses. They would apparently be sheltered there until the new barracks were built. My feet would trick me like this: unmindfully, they would lead me to our houses, and I would stare at them from a distance, wondering what was going on inside. I knew that the commander was staying in our big room, and, believing that he would be cautious, I was not very worried about it. But I imagined the worst in relation to the other rooms; at times, I imagined their windows torn out, their glasses broken, the floor planks cracked, the shelves in pieces, or even the garret fallen down.

But that morning, I felt somehow calmer, because I saw that the soldiers had lit fires around our fountain in Topillo, on which they had put two large cauldrons and were washing clothes in them. It's good that they did not light it inside, or the houses could have burnt down, I thought to myself. '*Bring wood!*' Sergeant Hate shouted. The other, who obviously did not feel like going up to the pile of wood they kept behind the post, went to Uncle's field and grabbed the pivot with his bare arms, pulled it as if it were a willow birch stuck in clay, and threw it on the fire. He went back, took the fence sticks and thrust them under the second cauldron. 'With what are we going to thresh tomorrow?' I thought I was shouting as loud as I could, but I instantly realised that my voice was stuck in my throat and I could barely breathe. I was short of breath, as if all the air surrounding the field and the houses around had disappeared into the sky. Even the mountain air felt as if it was lost. I don't know where to. I crouched down and could hardly come to my senses, because I still had the same thought in my mind: *'With what is Uncle going to thresh tomorrow? Tomorrow…, the day after…, and the day after that…?'*

A women's song brought me to my senses. I remembered that it was a Monday and they were accompanying the new bride to fetch water for the first time from Topillo. It was the newest bride in the village, the one who got married to avoid going to action. This was an ancient custom in our village: after the wedding, the new bride was accompanied to the fountain with songs. There, she filled water for the first time, and she poured from that water for her husband, with whom she had slept with for the first time, so that he washed his face. With that same water, she also brewed coffee for her father-in-law and mother-in-law. All the brides of the village fetched the first water from Topillo, not only because it was the best in the seven provinces, but also because it was the first spring that those three women had found—centuries ago—when they left Gushaja to escape from that cursed disease that had plagued the whole village.

This fountain was the site of yet another custom of our weddings. On a small heap there, the cattle that would be consumed by the wedding guests were slaughtered. Not because there were no other places to slaughter the wedding ox, calf or cow, but because before the blade was thrust, they would always take the animal to drink water from Topillo, not with songs of women and brides, but with drums and pipes that played a distinct tune even for the slaughter of the calf. This had always astonished me; the drums and pipes played distinct tunes not only for the dances of women or men, or for the dancing of young boys or young girls, but also for everything else that took place during the wedding days, from the moment they reached the Upper Hill and started the celebration with: 'Omer Aga, hipi kalit dhe eja në shtëpi se nusen ta kanë martuar, shtëpinë ta kanë djegur, fëmijët t'i kanë përzënë…'[49], or with 'Vijnë pamporat, moj nanë, bregut të detit,

---

[49] 'Omer Aga, ride a horse and come home, as they married off your bride, burned down your house, drove away your children…'

o seç po vijnë asqerët e mbretit…'[50] A distinct tune for when the groom and his best man would gather the brides and girls invited to the wedding from every house; when the father-in-law, along with the dressmakers, left to take the bridal gown to the bride; when the groom went to the bride's house at sunrise with drums and pipes to wake her up from her last girlish sleep; and also for the horse race that took place early in the morning, before the departure of the kinship who would accompany the bride. This one was a fast melody that suited the rhythm of horseshoes on the cobblestones. I got closer to better hear the young women embroidering their words for the new bride so beautifully, while she walked as if in a dream, with two kettles in hand. When they approached the fountain, a loud 'hurraaaay!' that scared me was heard. 'What is it?' Seven or eight soldiers, who were washing their clothes around the fountain, had gathered together and cheered, as they made all kinds of gestures towards the bride. The women stopped the song. Intimidated, the new bride froze, whereas the two kettles now seemed to weigh as much as cannonballs. After a bit of confusion, the women started to sing again, but this time they no longer sang to the bride, but to the soldiers who shouted 'Hurraaay!', and made fun of them.

Shto çinite, bre askeri, takvo çudo?
Dal ste doshle bre askeri, ot shumishta,
Ot shumishta, bre askeri, ot dolishta?
Taja nije, bre askeri, milmllanesta,
I ne nije, bre askeri, xhambalishta!

When they finished the song, they left and took the bride, for the first time in seven centuries, to fill water in the well of the Kulics, two or three houses away. 'Come here,' Sergeant Hate shouted, smirking at me. He was a hawk-nosed man with downturned eyes, the most sinister among the sergeants of the border post. His misdeeds were spoken of so widely that, when little children cried, they're not told 'stop' a monster is heard, but 'stop, Hate will come!' I approached timidly, because every time I saw Hate, I remembered the day he pointed his rifle at me and fired it, amused by my fear; as my knees knocked in fear, his moustache shook with the pleasure of having terrified a child as if it were a rabbit.

---

[50] 'The steamers are reaching the sea shore, o mother, that's the king's soldiers coming…'

'Come here, I said!' he shouted once more. 'What did those women say in their song? Was it about us?' About us, as they mentioned the word 'askeri, askeri' four times. Or does it have any other meaning?'

'No, it means soldier.'

'And what did they say about us?'

'I didn't get all the words,' I replied.

I was scared to say that the women's song said: What is this oddity you are up to, o soldiers, have you come from the woods, or from the streams' scarps, This is, o soldiers, our beloved bride, and she's not, O soldiers, a carnival to laugh at!

'Tell me what you understood!' the sergeant ordered.

They said, 'Have you ever laid your eyes on a bride, or not?'

'Is it so? Get lost!'

'This is my fountain!' I was taken aback by my own words. Where did they come from? Why did they leave my mouth?

'Whaat?' Sergeant Hate looked at me as if I had sprouted from that rocky ground, five steps away from Topillo, that very instant. 'Get lost, I said!'

I turned around and slowly walked to where the women's song for the young bride attracted me. They were returning and the drops of water, falling from the two kettles in the hands of the new bride, to me, seemed like women's tears.

28

In the afternoon, all of a sudden, the sky turned dark. The ominous sound of the wind seemed to come out of the ground. The clouds over Gjallica grew furious and moved towards Maja e Zezë. Over our village, they collided with cloud pieces they found there—the leftovers of several days—and moved in the direction of the Kollovoz Mountain again, and then over Kallabak and Murga. The sound of the wind moving through the heights resembled the howl of rabid dogs. 'They'll be stranded!' Grandma said, very worried. 'They are risking life and limb for a lamb!' she added harshly. It seemed like the best moment to ask, and I found out why the whole village council had been summoned to the Locality.

Four days ago, our forest guard had caught a man and a woman cutting beech leaves without permission. He had taken the man's axe and the woman's headscarf, telling them that the items would be returned only after they paid the fine. 'Do you know who I am?' the man called from behind. 'Even if you are the son of God, you have to pay the fine,' the guard replied and left for the village. 'I am the father of Security!' the man shouted and this time, the guard shivered. For years, the word "Security" made people tremble in fear, causing them a strange tremor under their skin, a tangled movement of the body hair, and they couldn't even tell where it came from, other than from a dreary night. But the guard had said his words, and he could command neither his mind nor his feet to go back. '*If a word leaves the mouth, it becomes a chain and ties you,*' he thought to himself. Instead, he said: 'When you come to pay the fine, I will find out who you are.'

'You will regret this!' In the evening, someone from the Locality came and asked the council for the headscarf and the axe. 'They should pay the fine first,' Uncle said. He had been elected councillor that year, nominated by some village elders and not by the organisation. 'Do you know who they belong to?' the

Locality representative exclaimed. 'Do they not belong to God himself?' Uncle replied in the words of the forest ranger.

But when they came to learn that the headscarf belonged to the mother of the Locality secretary and the axe to the father of the Security officer in the province centre, the councillors split in two; half wanted to give them their belongings to avoid trouble, while the others objected, saying that if we gave it to them with no fine, kiss goodbye to the forest! They threw it in the ballot and the vote came out equal, so the representative of the Locality left without being able to take the headscarf and the axe. About three days later, the councillors and the guard were summoned to explain themselves.

'They will be stranded,' Grandmother repeated, and, as if her words were an order from heaven, the windows shook as all the walls of the house felt the bite of an exceptional gust. The snow, the rain, the wind and the darkness combined turned that afternoon and the following night into a corner of hell on earth. 'They will be stranded,' Grandmother repeated for the third time. 'Seven men will be sacrificed for an axe and a headscarf.' All those present in the room kept silent, while the threatening cries of that savage storm were heard in the house. I don't know for how long we stood like that, wrapped in a nightmarish anxiety. Yet, eventually, Father came and announced that they had been sheltered at friends in the Locality for fear of the storm and that they'd be back after the storm was gone.

In the morning, the storm, exhausted from a long night, had rested over Gjallica and Maja e Zezë, but the snowfall was so intense that the first thing the men of the village decided to do was to remove the snow from the roofs so that it didn't break the beams and hurt the people in the houses. I went to the window countless times. I stared at the spot across the river, where the path from the Locality passed. Everything was covered in snow, and the hills or mountain peaks looked like giant eggs, like those in the tales of Scheherazade that Anatolia told me. As the lunch table was about to be set, someone shouted, 'They're coming!' Indeed, they were coming, but it was not our seven councillors, but a long line of countless men. 'What could it be?' Everybody ran to Kodra e Poshtme[51], from where the path could be seen more clearly, and noticed that the line of men walking slowly through the waist-deep snow was carrying seven people in stretchers. The matching of the number of stretchers with that of our

---

[51] The Lower Hill

130

seven councillors terrified the whole village; the women started weeping whereas the kids dived in and got stuck in snow.

Five or six young men set out to clear the way with their feet and chests and to meet the men. When they eventually met and learned the truth, one of them hurried back and brought some relief along with quite tragic news: 'They are not ours; they are seven soldiers who froze at the border.'

'C'mon men, let's join forces; it's on us to take them to Orgosta.' No one, neither the women nor children, moved away until the men carrying the seven soldiers wrapped in large rugs, arrived. All I could utter amid that overwhelming silence was:

'Are they dead?'

'No, they froze,' someone replied, and between my question and the answer I received, there was neither life nor death, just hope.

When one of my aunts, who happened to be among the women, came and wiped my tears, I realised that I had been crying silently. And when our men, four by four, took the seven soldiers in their arms, a woman touched the rugs in pain and said:

'They froze like birds. This winter wiped out the beech buds!'

Following her words, three other women started wailing aloud. The soldiers were carried through the middle of the village, in a mournfully white silence. I went and told Majka everything, because she had not gone out, as she had no power to walk through the heavy snow.

'They froze stretching the telephone wire in the plains,' I told her.

'Who knows where God was yesterday, to have left the poor birds in the hands of the storm!' she said and, after a while, with her mind racing, she asked: 'Are there no wireless telephones?' I was upset that Majka said silly things, and I didn't know how to answer that odd question of hers. 'How could telephones be wireless? What's this Majka of ours thinking?'

For three days in a row, nobody talked about anything else other than the seven soldiers. When I saw the soldiers in the village—the ones that had occupied our houses—they seemed completely innocent to me, and I feared that one day, they too could freeze over Maja e Zezë, which was even colder than Kallabak and Murga. It was only Hate whom I would not feel sorry for, and I didn't want to tell anybody the reason.

131

29

On the fourth day, the topic of the unstoppable flow of conversation, whining and gossip changed. Two policemen from the Locality came to the village and took away the forest guard in chains. Our councillors had quarrelled and had refused to hand over the kerchief and the axe. At first, they were divided, but when the Security officer came to defend his father's axe and started cursing and threatening, the councillors agreed on one thing: 'Without paying the fine, the headscarf and the axe won't be returned!'

'You will see who I am!' the officer threatened and left, slamming the door as if he were the son of that day's storm.

When the police took the guard, some of the councillors ran to defend him, but they returned crestfallen. The head of the Locality, without shouting and in a calm voice, had told them: 'We didn't want to make a big deal out of this. You asked for it. Your guard is being arrested because he wanted to assault the Locality secretary's mother. This is why he took her headscarf, and, when our officer's father went to protect her, he took his axe. You better put an end to this mess and the guard gets off with only one month in prison, not more!' All the councillors, just like the whole village, knew the guard well and could swear on their lives that this was not true, but who would have ears for their oath? 'Don't play with fire, water and those in power!' Grandmother said again to Uncle, who was venting more than actually talking to anyone. One morning, I saw him throwing two big bowls of corn in a sack and leaving his house. I followed him to see where he would take it. He knocked on the door of the guard and handed them the sack of corn, so that the children left with no father were fed.

But the guard was kept in prison for only seven days. As the saying goes: everything wears out by thinning, only oppression by thickening. And the oppression towards our village, at the time, had thickened a lot. Our forest was cut down; our councillors were stepped on; our guard was chained up; and as if all these were not enough, one day, Sergeant Hate along with another beat and bruised my uncle beyond reason.

He had gone to the forest to cut wood, to replace the pivot and the fence holders that the soldiers had taken. 'Why are you cutting wood at the post's share?' Sergeant Hate threatened. 'It belongs to us, not to the post!' he replied. 'Who made it for you?'

'My grandfather, great-grandfather, and his great-grandfather. Who else?' Uncle resisted. Hate snatched a freshly cut thick beech branch while the other used the butt of the rifle to hit Uncle mercilessly as they pushed him towards the border.

The beech branch whistled on his back; the rifle butt hammered, but Uncle did not feel it; he was seized by an even more terrible fright when he noticed that they were leading him towards the soft belt…'*They'll kill me and put shame on my name, by claiming I wanted to flee,*' he thought. Ever since the story of aspirant Shefqet and the soldiers killed at the border spread, everyone was terrified of being tricked in that way.

He was lucky. At that moment, the other patrol came and took him under its protection. 'Leave him to us. We caught him!' Sergeant Hate shouted. 'Your shift is over; now it's our turn', the one in charge of the second shift said. Hate left infuriated. The whole village was perturbed. My beaten uncle was visited by several kins, friends, neighbours; some female relatives also brought him "*sahan*"[52]. This is what we used to say when someone was visited with a copper *sahan*—one of those from the time of the Turks—which was full of pancakes or *fli* prepared for those who had been released from the hospital or prison, for those who had come back from emigration or the army, or in case of other similar occasions of a rural life. I had also recently heard that some of the granddaughters married off at various places had visited their grandfather Arif with *sahans* of pancakes and *fli*, just because he had decided to grow a beard. 'Why?' I asked Majka. 'When a man decides to grow a beard, he has decided to talk to the sky rather than the earth,' she said. The visits with *sahan* in the hands of women also sensitised the men who visited Uncle, so that even Salko spoke in defence of his fellow villager.

When Majka came to heal his wounds with her herbs and said: 'I will heal the wounds of this unfortunate, but who will heal the village? Are you, who Hate has placed under his thumb, even men?' their blood boiled. Altogether, they got

---

[52] A big decorated metal plate

up and went to the post commander and, the next day, three or four among them went to the Locality, then to the city, to the chiefs of the army and to the committee with a balcony and to the one without any. About five days later, a lieutenant colonel along with two civilians from both committees came to the village. They summoned the four soldiers of the two border guard shifts in front of the men of the village, and they told the truth. Even Hate confessed to what he had done, although he looked at the people like a wounded sable. 'What did you hit him with?' the lieutenant colonel asked him. 'With a branch,' Hate said. 'What about you?'

'With the butt of a rifle.'

'Tie them both!' the lieutenant colonel ordered. 'Take them to the Commander's Office immediately!' The councillors also told him about the axe and the headscarf. He shook his head but did not say a word, yet the following evening, the forest guard was back home.

30

After finishing grade four, I had almost no friends left in the village; the two I was the closest with—Halil and Braçe—went to Tirana. The first to his brother and the latter to his father who worked as confectioners and who were famous in the capital that called them "Gega". There, they started middle school; they went to "Ali Demi". A cousin of mine had also gone to the lyceum of Tirana, because he drew very well. The others, either older or younger than me, had their own crews and I was left almost alone. From time to time, the King's Son would come and call on me. Although he was three years older, since he was slow-witted, he seemed younger and for some reason, he liked my company. Probably because I was the only one who listened to him chatter without interrupting him, or because I made him whistles out of wheat straw and spruce stalks, which he blew as he went through the village streets, believing that he was a musician. He came early also that morning and called on me, and, from the way he murmured and twisted his hands, it seemed he wanted to tell me some secret that he thought he was the only one to know.

'Hey', I made fun of him as soon as I saw him, 'what is three times three?'

'Six, I have told you a thousand times, six. No other way around.'

He quickly explained that he had discovered where Sabah and Abdil set their traps to catch quail. They were two grown boys who worked as carpenters in the city, but in the winter, they were on leave and caught quail with baskets. The King's Son and I had tried to make one too, but our mechanism was nothing like theirs: the bottom not flat enough, the cover not round enough. And now, the King's Son was telling me where their basket was, so that we could take it and set it up somewhere for our own account. I did not think twice, and we left.

We found the basket in an alder forest; we took it and set it on another spot. To me, it was the wonderful work of two carpenters. It was woven of willow and rested on a vertical stick, which, in turn, horizontally held a shovel, also woven of willow twigs and rye straw, and on which they put baked oat grains. More oats were left out of the basket to attract the birds with their smell. When the quail pushed on the shovel, it triggered the basket to fall and catch the quails inside.

'We won't catch anything,' I told the King's Son, as we set the basket up at another juniper grove, 'No quail will come here.'

On our way back, the first person we met started shouting and yelling at me: where were you, where did you go, what the hell are you doing? We have been looking for you everywhere. I was taken aback and could not understand why they sought me, but I was quickly told that the men of the village were leaving for the mountains for the trial to settle the border with the other village.

I rushed to my grandmother to get the oldest and most beautiful Koran in the village, the only one that had been brought from Mecca. She was waiting for me with two bags in hand, the embroidered one, where she kept the Koran and an ordinary bag, where she had prepared me some bread, cottage cheese and two or three apples,—the leftovers of that hungry winter that was hardly passing although the first days of April were here.

The men of the village had gathered in front of the cafe, making a real mess. They shouted, cursed, gathered and whispered in groups, and it wasn't clear why they were being so loud.

'I will come too, you can't go without me!' Stalin shouted, his cheeks flushed, overshadowing the red of his hair. 'It's the Party which decides on everything.'

'When the Party gives birth to any highland, let it decide on that,' Uncle told him.

After a while, I came to understand why they were arguing: those who wanted to take from our highlands had asked for seven elders that would swear by bread and salt, with their hand on the Koran, for the border of the highland. One of the appointed elders had left for the city and the other party had given an ultimatum: if even one of the seven elders is not present, the meadows of Bajram Luli—which were the lands being disputed over—would be left to them. The village paid Uko, as the fastest, to go to town and bring the missing elder back. He did not go through Maja e Gjarprit[53] like all villagers did, but took the shortcut through Gryka e Vanave, where the three rivers—the Reka of Borje, the Reka of Topojan and the Reka e Orgosta—came together. He crossed the river several times, both to the right and to the left, whenever the path went through the creeks

---

[53] Serpent's Peak

of the gorge and raging waters. It was a dangerous thing to do, so the words 'Uko Nana, ne idi po Vana' (Uko Nana, do not go through Vana) were said. And as the seventh among the elders of the village was still missing, Salko kept shouting: 'The day will come for you to ask the Party for the highlands, but it will be too late.'

'You know what; he is right,' a man said, 'Why do they want a piece of our highland? Because they have it all: in the war, it is them; in the Committee, it is them; in the council, them again; in the Locality, them…in the Security, them, also them in the police. This is why they want to toy with us.'

'The girls of Bukojna to action,' added another.

'And so on!' shouted one of those present.

'And so forth!' said a third one.

'So why not take the Party with us?' asked the first.

'Because this party of ours would cooperate with their party and leave us with only half of the highland', Uncle cried, enraged. And, as they did not agree, they decided to take Salko along, but on the condition that some others would accompany him.

'You want to spy on me? Koçi Xoxe's time, when the Party was being spied on, is over,' Salko said, raising his head. In an attempt to seem like more than he really was, this was how he puffed his chest, but his chin protruded past it.

'You spy on us all year long; we only get one day.'

Again, a mess of words and movement ensued. Yet, within the prevailing chaos, we set off for the mountains.

'Watch out,' Father told me, as he helped me mount the mule and fastened the saddle straps; he didn't want to come. I didn't reply. Instead I secured the Koran bag on the saddle swell. I was at the end, so I could watch that assorted bunch in front of me; some on foot and some riding, they had set out to defend what was rightfully theirs: our highland, which in the years that are not remembered, had been washed by a woman with tears and with fire. Her little son had left the house to go to the forest to pick strawberries, but he had not returned. They had searched for him for days but could not find him. Months later, his mother, who would go to the forest every day to look for him, found a torn piece of a shirt and recognised it because she had knitted it herself. 'My only son was swallowed by the forest!' she wailed and returned home. She took all the straw and dry grass in the house, and also took from the straw of her kin, and scattered it to the four corners of the forest. With a burning torch, she set them on fire. The forest burned for three weeks, until there were no signs of wood, wolf, fox, weasel, bear or rabbit. But even after that, the poor woman continued to wander with a lit torch in hand. She was found frozen on a winter morning at Kroi i Kuq[54]. Years later, green grass began to grow over the black ashes and the scorched forest turned into our highland.

Our village had been involved in a dispute regarding the highland even before the war, but at the time, it was with Novoseja, which, leaning on the Bajraktar, wanted to get parts from the Kallabak highland of Bukojna as well as from the highland of Brekinja. Novoseja produced several witnesses—it is unknown whether they had been paid or intimidated—while Bukojna submitted a very old legal decision dated "Rebyil-level 1252", and written in Turkish. The Civil Court of the Prefecture of Kosovo, based in Prizren, on June 28, 1937, granted the right of the highland to our village 'starting from the Guri i Ngulun[55], in the field of Kurt Aga, straightforward to the thin path that goes through the birch forest and to Guri Jeshil[56] and from there to the Kajnak (the spring) and further to the narrow road to Shkrepi i Kallabakut[57]...' I knew these places well, because, when the cattle were in the highlands, every three weeks, we would go to feed them salt and bran, which we would either throw on the highland slabs or feed it to them directly from the bags.

However, at a time when the Bajraktar's power waned, Novoseja let us be, and the trouble with the other village commenced. All those "little bajraktars" who worked in committees and councils had grown up there. I had heard that immediately after the war, a commander of the Serbian partisans went to one of the villages of Kosovo, on the outskirts of Gora, between Dragash and Prizren and in broad daylight, looted all the belongings that the emigrated sons of a lonely old woman had sent her from Istanbul. 'What are you doing?' the old woman cried 'And you call yourself liberators!'

'Majko,' the Serb replied to her, 'koj te osllobodill, toj i te jebill!'[58]

Instinctively, I tightly clutched the Koran that was on the saddle. Mother's only brother had brought it from Mecca, where he had gone for Hajj; this is why they requested it for special events and oaths. The imams had asked my

---

[54] Red Spring

[55] Pinned Stone

[56] Green Stone

[57] Crag of Kallabak

[58] Who liberates you has also screwed you

grandmother several times to keep it in the mosque, as it was an exceptional Koran, but she had told them it was safer in her house than in theirs. There was also another reason for her refusal to give it to anyone: it was the most precious souvenir from her only son, who was lost.

The voice of Uncle, who gave me some pieces of paper, shook me to my senses: 'Put them inside the Koran and don't show them to anyone. Did you hear me?' I managed to read just what was written on top of them: Legal Decision. In the name of His Majesty, Zog the 1ˢᵗ, King of Albanians, By the will of the people…'*The trial for the highland*,' I thought, and imagined the king the same as the King's Son, with whom I had stolen the quail basket that morning; no other image would come to my mind as I had never seen any pictures of the real king.

31

When we were quite close to the highland, an officer with two soldiers stopped us. Only seven will pass, the officer said, the others go back!

'I am from the Party!' Salko was the first to complain.

'The Party we have here is more than enough,' the officer said.

Our villagers took these words wrong and considered them threats, so, revolted, they started objecting. Some got off their horses; some others started shouting from atop the saddles.

'Listen, men' the commander shouted, 'I don't know if you know me, I am from Mirdita!'

'Even if you were Bardhok Biba's grandson, so what?' a short man from the Isaacs neighbourhood cried; on the only gramophone the village had, they would listen to Bardhok Biba's song every day.

'No, pal, don't assume airs! I am the grandson of Gjin Ndoi, the shepherd of Perlat, killed for the highlands of Kumbulla. I don't want anybody else to be killed for a highland border. Did you hear me, you, the one that jumps like a rooster?'

Silence. None of our men had set out to be killed in the mountains on that day…

'This is why I am telling you,' the officer continued, 'seven among you and seven among them. No guns!'

'He seems to be a good person,' I heard Olloman say to the man next to him. He was one of the seven appointed to take the oath, not only because of his age, but also because everyone knew him as a wise man, respectful to order, true to his word.

'He is good only if he puts the others in order too, so that they do not come along with the Security', the man next to Olloman replied. One of them, the "Security", a tubby man wearing a beret, moved around, but did not get too close to us. Everyone knew he wore a gold chain watch, which had once belonged to a young man from our village and who was found murdered at Çesmja e Hanës[59], only three weeks after his wedding.

They eventually made arrangements with the officer to allow nine of us to go further: the seven elders, me who would hold the Koran and Uncle, because, as the officer was told, 'he records all the important events that occur in the village and this is not a minor one.'

'I hope it does not get any bigger,' the officer said. Upon those words, Uko Nana along with the elder appointed to swear on behalf of our village appeared. We left, while the others remained there to wait for us. We went to the meeting place and after a while, the men of the other village came. They were also nine, but there were no children like myself among them. They too had brought a Koran along, but Olloman told them that they would take the oath solely on the one, in the whole province, that had come from Mecca. 'Very well,' they said, 'but you will perform ablution before our eyes.'

'I know what the matter is,' Olloman told them. 'You want to check our *opinga*?' It was said that someone had taken a false oath somewhere in a meadow bush. He had placed dirt from his yard into his *opinga* and then, claiming 'I swear on my faith and belief, I am standing on my own land,' he had obtained the entire meadow from the other. They all took off their shoes and performed ablution, murmuring prayers so that their oath would be valid.

'We came looking for our right, not for upheaval,' Olloman said, as he gazed towards the highland, not the men gathered there. He secured his *opinga* and rose powerfully.

'Come on, bring the Koran,' said one of the men of the other village, when we approached a ravine, 'Put it here on the grass.'

'Not there,' I said, 'the Koran rests on this big stone which was here three hundred years before us and will be here three hundred years after. Grass dries and rots, stone doesn't.'

Everyone looked at me in astonishment, and Olloman put his hand on my shoulder. I placed the Koran on Guri Jeshil, put a piece of wheat bread and a little salt on it and cried: 'Ready!' Olloman was the first to talk and he said these words: 'On the Koran, this bread and salt, vallahi…bilahi…tallahi…I swear on my highland not to bother anyone, and whoever tries to take what is rightfully mine, may he get his in this world and in the hereafter!' The other men swore as well, and we departed; Olloman first, I behind him and the others after me.

---

[59] The Hana Fountain

Olloman walked and continued to swear: 'On the Koran, this bread and salt, where we are stepping on is the border of our highland…On the Koran, this bread and salt…'

We walked along the field of Kurt, through a path above the forest, towards the small stream. Then, we walked in the stream, treading through the water, as the water was shared, and then we took the direction of the small stream. The men of the other village started to leave and the only one left among them said that we were to continue to the spot where the two streams met, because the land ahead of us was not subject to dispute. But we kept going and reached Çezma e Mbretit[60] and, then Guri i Prerë[61] and finally Plehu i Spahisë[62]. Later, we left the highland and went to the village to write some documents, but we didn't see any of the seven men of the other village; nobody could tell us where they were. 'Weren't they in the mountains with you?' a woman asked and, when we told her everything that had happened, she left murmuring something…We did not get if she was cursing us, or the men of her village.

As we were about to head home, a mountain shepherd came. Frightened and with a trembling voice, he told us: 'Olloman's ox bloated!' His eyes were gloomy, but he calmly told us to hurry to the village and gather ivy branches and leaves near the Dobrajca quarries, and, with them, crown the horns of the cows and calves. For centuries, the people of my village believed that the leaves of this plant, which twisted around the stones, could ward off evil from the pen.

'The bogeyman reached the highlands,' Olloman said, 'only the crown of ivy can scare it off.'

---

[60] King's Fountain
[61] The Cut Stone
[62] Spahi's Dung

32

The more St George's Day approached, the more often people asked: 'Will the girls come, will they be allowed back at least for St George, or will the only ones given permission be those whose parents are in the council and organisation and those whose uncles are civil servants? This was the topic of conversation everywhere, because everybody was aware that without girls there could be no St George's. This had always been the case, since the sun rose over Maja e Zezë. 'Without the girls, even the flowers of St George won't bloom,' I had once heard Grandmother Ajnurka say, and I kept repeating it while chatting with others. However, nobody knew the answer. As soon as one claimed that they would come, another suggested that they could not come without finishing the work they had started, and yet another exclaimed that they would not be given permission on St George's, as the newspapers in Tirana had started writing against backwards customs and considered St George as such; somebody else, who pretended to be even more well-read remarked that they would not come, because on St George's Day, Enver Hoxha would go to action to meet our girls. Too many words: unsieved, unsifted.

Some of the men—and even I—asked Teacher. He gave no answer. I had come to notice that starting from the last conference for the action, when the main delegate talked to him menacingly, Teacher was more silent and went to the café less often. I had seen him sitting for hours at the window of his room perplexed and gazing at the mountain mist, which had become thicker and greyer, the colour of wolf pelt. However, the mist in Teacher's eyes scared me more. Hence, I did not dare to ask him questions like before, especially after I heard from someone that the delegate's threats were in relation to his father, who had been executed on the first days after liberation. 'That's why they brought him here amidst our mountains and fogs. It was because of his poor biography, not in vain.'

Whether the girls would come for St George's became less certain with every passing day; the certainly true news that one of the girls—Zumreta—was killed in action, hit the village like a bomb...

Her mother, grandfather and a little sister lived in our village, whereas her father had remained isolated in a town of Bosnia, after the border with the neighbouring state was closed and the soldiers on either side did not permit even the sparrows to cross. They were notified to go to town and they left joyful, in the hope that the emigrant would have sent them money or any parcels. But when they got there, they found the girl in a coffin. Several speeches were held in front of the Committee with a balcony, and, then, the poor girl was taken to the martyrs' cemetery. On the way to the village café, I heard someone say that the newspaper had also written about this event; the girl of our village had been called a little heroine. Yet, before her family returned from the funeral ceremony, we came to learn the news that Zumreta had not died working heroically, but because she contracted lice typhoid fever.

Fear struck every household that had sent their girls to action. Majka sent for me and I went to her right away, because I loved that old woman who seemed to come from a foreign, unknown world. But she looked at me with a strange curiosity as well, as if she would find her forgotten childhood in me.

'You will take me to Fshati i Priftit,' she told me.

I did not hesitate. I took our quiet mule, helped her get on it, and we left. She had taken a big jug of water along, and, when we got there, she put it on the groundsel blackened by the candles that had been lit over time, whispered a few words while looking up at the sky and then, we headed back. I didn't ask her what she was up to and what she had in mind, for I knew her nature and that she never wanted to reveal her secret whispers. When we reached the village, she put the water amid the rubble of the Burnt Mosque, whispered something there too, and went inside her house, telling me to wait for her. She came out with a small washtub and a bunch of celosia, a flower with crimson tassels and dense leaves, which in other villages was also called cockscomb, probably because of its crimson colour.

'Where are we going?' I dared to ask.

'To the seven gates,' she told me and started walking down the main road of the village.

She stopped in front of Murat's gate, pierced by the bullets of those who, many years ago, kidnapped a girl from our village and put her in a goat wool sack. She ordered me to pour some water from the jug into the small washtub, put the handful of celosia inside, and, mumbling those words that only she knew and understood, sprinkled the big gate with water. My eyes were fixed on the water droplets, which fell on the holes of the olden bullets.

'Let's go to the next gate,' Majka told me. And we performed this rite at all the seven gates of the village; where the girls would once gather and sing. At each gate, the crowd of people who noticed and began to quietly follow her grew larger. By the time we reached the last gate, enough people to fill the two mosques of our village—both that of the Lower Neighbourhood and that of the Upper Neighbourhood, which was already languishing in charred rubbles—had gathered. When we were at the last gate, an absentminded Salko joined us too, his nose as red as *ajvár*[63]...

'What is this forgotten woman doing?' She did not answer, nor did she pay any heed to him. Yet, when she was done, in a metallic voice that I had never heard before, I heard Majka say:

'I am trying to save the girls from evil!'

'Ah what a good laugh; you hag, there is no God to hear you!' Salko said.

'Everyone's god is in his soul. You go by yours; I, by mine. May God save you too!' said Majka and sprinkled him with the celosia bunch.

'Keep playing with the washtub, go on,' Salko said angrily.

'The nightingale and the cuckoo may sing on the same day, but not the same song, Bukojna's redhead,' Majka replied. Salko's expression darkened and he wanted to say something. Yet, upon seeing that the crowd was ready to storm at him in case he "drew his sword", he kept his mouth shut. When he was about to leave, someone from behind called out to him: Cock, cockscomb, a bitch bell! It suited him well, as he would pry into everything with his jingles. He did not turn his head back, but his ringing would be heard the following day. Early in the morning, two police officers came from the Locality and took Majka to interrogate her at the state offices. The brides of the household freaked out and pretty soon, everybody came to learn that Majka had been arrested by the Locality police. Some of Majka's grandsons, as well as many boys and men, did not leave her alone; they marched for two hours to reach the offices.

'Shame on you,' cried one of our men, 'you tied an old woman up and you're putting on airs!'

---

[63] A traditional condiment made with red bell peppers and eggplants

All of us stood in front of the offices of the Locality, even though the two policemen wanted us to disband. Majka was not held for more than half an hour; in the meantime, many villagers from the Locality centre joined us and asked surprised:

'What? Why did they tie her up? What did she do?'

'She has spoken to God,' replied Olloman America. At that moment, they were taking Majka out of the offices and the Head of the Locality, a broad handsome man, either because he heard these words or because of the words he exchanged with Majka, roared at her in a thick voice:

'And remember well, to us, god is Enver Hoxha!'

'You have your own god, son, I have mine,' she answered and set off to get on the mule.

33

As Majka tried to save the girls with water blessed in the church and the mosque, no one gave a second thought to the village boys who looked even worse; they were tortured by the absence of the girls; they longed for their songs at the seven gates of the village and for the scent of flowers; they wandered through the dull streets, they had become peevish and quarrelsome. The ridicule from men, and occasionally some woman, had begun to weigh on them more than many other things. Nefka, or as we had started to call her, the 'village newspaper', spread her noise at any fountain or behind any fence so zealously that one of the youngsters once told her: 'If you don't shut up, I will tie you up at Druri i Vetmuar, and leave you there for the ground flies to feed on you.'

Nobody knew what the truth was, but it was said that the very same youngster that threatened Nefka, entered a house one day and found its hostess busy preparing the bread she was going to bake that day. She talked to him, but couldn't move because her hands were busy kneading the dough in the bowl. 'What do you want?' she asked him. 'I want you,' the youngster replied, lowering her clothes in a hurry, almost breathlessly, and he did what he intended to do. Poor woman found herself in a tight spot between shame and the bread she was holding in her hands. It seems that she preferred to save the bread so as not to leave the people of her household hungry and endured until the young man vented all his yearning for one of the action girls, or maybe for all of them. A few days later, as he wandered through the village streets, the dough woman gestured at him and he got inside.

'Fool,' she said, 'why did you want to do it near a dough bowl, when you could do it in bed?' He was startled, both by this incident as well as by a flame of pleasure that took hold of him as he watched the woman undress, and, when she crawled in bed, he jumped over her in a tearing hurry. 'Slow down, slow down,' the woman said, 'let me touch and see what God has given you to give us women.' She grabbed him, rubbed it a little till she noticed the boy revel in pleasure, and as fast as a wild goat of the Brod Mountains, she pulled a bread knife from under her pillow, cutting off what in those few moments had grown in her hand. The room was flooded with screams, the bed with blood; the boy ran away frightened, whereas the woman shouted at him from behind: 'Do not soil someone else's bread, you filthy being!'

This story spread throughout the entire village, but nobody mentioned the name of the woman who had done the unspeakable, and no one could say for sure if this event was true, or another one of the 'village newspaper's' lies, who broadcasted news behind fences every single day. One of her news was that some youngsters had started harassing little schoolgirls—and some even boys—who they called behind stacks to give them candy from the café, to teach them to smoke or even to masturbate. True or not, parents became more vigilant and spent their days trying to gather and keep an eye on their children, girls and boys alike.

'When will this cursed action—that withered our girls and drove our boys crazy—be over,' they would say, talking to themselves more so than to others.

Majka got very angry at that chatterbox, Nefka, when she badmouthed one of her grandsons. She went to her yard and spoke harshly to her. 'Nefka, you falcon who goes hand in hand with the devil,' she told her. But Nefka did not sit still for it and, shouting from the porch where she was shredding corn, she said: 'Get out of my yard you trot or I will send my dogs to tear you to pieces.' It was as if lightning struck Majka, and she verbalised all the words that could be said to a woman in such cases; from witch to falcon and virago, from slut to trollop and hussy, and from minger and moo to harridan and tart. Still on the porch, Nefka let out thunders of her own and got inside only when Majka raised her stick, calling: 'Get out of my sight you basement spy!'

It was my misfortune that I happened to see and hear things that, had Nefka learned, she would have astonished not only our village, but the whole province between the two Drin Rivers and the three Mountains. One evening, I was checking the barn roofs to find where the sparrows hid, when I noticed him! It was the very same boy I had seen the day before the action on the straw with the girl whose name I never learned. He walked around the barn, and, with a wire brush, he rubbed a beautiful, young female colt, fed her grass, scratched her lightly on the forehead and between the ears, and combed her mane, hugging her. I was not surprised, because in our village everyone loves horses and, on every wedding or Saint George's, races—which are truly entertaining events for the people and of which is talked about till the next race—are held. What took me aback was his song:

'Moj e mira te murrizi,
Bjermi cicat t'i qëndisi,
Ojna, ojna, pa gjylpanë,
Rreth e m'rreth t'i kaç me dhamë.'[64]

Yet my eyes nearly popped out of my head when I saw that enormous man take off his pants and raise the colt's tail. Still incapable to breathe from what I was witnessing, I heard him groan, just like the day before the action. I felt disgusted and inadvertently spat. 'Whoever you are, just let me be!' he cried, groaning, and I ran away. Where could I go?

I didn't want to see anyone for fear that I would let something slip or that someone from my family caught wind of anything and a dinner of unanswered questions, which bothered me deeply, would commence. I walked away from our yard, but, heck, Mother was collecting the dried laundry and called me.

'I am going to Anatolia, for fairy tales,' I told her from afar and hurried my step. She did not stop me as she knew my insatiable desire to listen to tales. However, nobody in my house told tales; women and men alike were so obsessed with housework and the words 'who cares about fairy tales in wicked times like these' were always on the tips of their tongues. Similarly, neither of my grandmothers told fairy tales. Occasionally, Mother would give us permission to call over our cousin Salifa, who kept us up all night recounting her grandmother's tales.

But the most beautiful tales of all were told by Anatolia, a plump Turkish woman, who had married a man from our village. He had taken her along when the Empire crumbled and, as soon as he reached the village, he took her to his bed and married her. Nobody took the trouble to learn her name; everyone called her Anatolia. She gave birth to a son, but her husband died soon after, and she got by and raised her son with embroideries and by teaching the women of the village how to cook Turkish dishes, *imambayildi*, sour milk casserole, juices of

---

[64] 'O the beauty by the hawthorn,
Let me embroider your tits,
Purling with no needle,
All around I'll nip them with my teeth'

forest fruit, and so on. She was also the one who taught everyone in the village how to preserve small white pears and apples for winter, by putting them in wooden vessels with water, in which they remained soft and unspoiled.

The water of apples was not for drinking, whereas that of pears was so yummy that when the Italian major—who came to our village before and during the war—tasted it, he said that it was very similar to champagne. None of us knew what champagne was, to tell if he was lying or telling the truth. Anatolia's son also died a few years after his son was born. And this one—the third generation—left the village when he got married. He worked somewhere far away and visited home once every three or six months. Some claimed that he was afraid of dying like his grandfather and father, others said that it was his wife who made him work in the city and buy a house there, as she did not intend to spend her life in this craphole of a village with those two old women who looked like two sisters abandoned by the fireplace. 'Even in heaven, two mothers-in-law are too big of a burden,' she would say of her husband's mother and grandmother. He, on the other hand, worked in a mine. It was said that when he was in Rubik, the two old women had asked their young daughter-in-law: 'When will you give us a son, dear daughter?'

The young woman had opened her arms and thighs in front of the fire of half rotten beeches that whistled like juniper birds and, looking at both of them angrily, had answered: 'It seems that you have lost your mind along with your falling hair. How can I have a son, if the pussy is in front of the fireplace and the dick in Rubik?'

Somebody who had worked in the mine with Anatolia's grandson for some time told the people in the village that he had lost his marbles once and forever, because of the ridicule from two engineers and a postwoman in Rubik. They taught him how to write a love letter to a dancer from the Tirana Ensemble who had performed for the mine workers those days. Anatolia's grandson, haunted by fantasies of the dancer's white arms and black eyelids, sent her several love letters, and all the time he received warm and promising answers, but it could not possibly have occurred to him that they were written by the two engineers and the postwoman. One day, he bought a new suit, shaved smooth and got ready to go to Tirana to meet the dancer, in accordance with the words written in the last letter he received. He thought he was so lucky when the two engineers told him that they would go to Tirana and offered him a ride. They also helped him find the dancer in the city, and, when she slapped him on the cheek, the two engineers laughed their heads off just a little further, as if they were watching a circus bear. The prank they played was learned throughout the mine; he went to the post office, called the postwoman a "Filthy bitch", and left for another job, of which nobody knew. He also started to visit the village less often.

34

Anatolia told Scheherazade's tales, which made me forget everything. I would become a different person and could not recognise myself. Whatever Anatolia asked of me, I would do; I helped her in all ways I could, and she was aware of my inexorable desire to listen to the tales of Scheherazade. I'd never go inside her house, if she did not invite me in; even when my thirst for a fairy tale was difficult to bear, I would sit under the window and wait for her to call me in. Recently, I had turned into Anatolia's only follower, because the others had left saying that they had heard these before, whereas I could listen to those tales ten times and still not have enough of them.

'Who told you these tales?' I once asked.

'My great grandpa,' she replied and said no more.

As I could not get what I saw in the barn out of my head, I stood under Anatolia's window that evening, too. Such things did not happen even in the tales of Scheherazade, who knew everything that happened in this world. It was getting dark and Anatolia had not yet opened the window to call me in. For the first time, I entered without being invited. That night, I had a burning desire for a fairy-tale, as I believed that it would put off that suffocating fire in my chest. When I went inside, I saw two other old women going from the room to the kitchen and back; they heated water, wet pieces of cloth in it, squeezed them, and went to the room with them in hand.

'Send that boy away, he is too young to see death with his own eyes!' one of the old women said.

'Anatolia is very sick,' her daughter in law told me.

But I did not move. I was afraid that if I left, I would not find Anatolia anymore. The two old women kept going back and forth murmuring, 'tawbah ar-Rab, tawbah ar-Rab,' and other words I did not understand. I don't know for how long I stood like that, but when I was capable of getting up, darkness had covered everything.

'You can't go anywhere at this hour,' the young daughter-in-law told me, 'the soldiers will catch you and keep you in the barracks all night, or even kill you as they killed your dog.'

I shivered in fear as she brought me bread and cottage cheese. 'Eat some,' she said 'and I will take you to bed.' The house lamps were all in Anatolia's room, as the old women who were trying to heal her needed them, and I stared at their silhouettes, reflected under the chimney flames. The bride, tall and delicate, with a bulging chest that strained the buttons of her vest to pop, looked even prettier, even taller. The glow from the fire made her white teeth look like pearls and her eyes gleam. She appeared to have emerged from the tales of Scheherazade.

She took me to her room, made my bed ready and went out saying: 'Rest, as we will be dealing with the old woman all night. I also sent word to your mother so that she doesn't worry.'

A few times, I woke up to the noise the two old women taking care of Anatolia made, and fell asleep again. For a moment—my eyes closed—I felt that the nostrils of my nose smelled a quince scent mixed up with another aroma I had never smelled before. The young daughter-in-law was in bed with me, and I don't know when she got there, but I am aware that I never had nor would I ever smell such a wonderful fragrance. It seemed to come from the quilt, the sheets, her shirt, the walls and ceiling of the room, from the sky and the ground, and filled my chest that had forgotten to breathe. I pretended to be sleeping. The bride turned on her side, put her hand under my neck, and asked me if I wanted to listen to her tale.

'Yes,' I said, dumbfounded and scared like a sparrow. 'My tale,' she said, 'is about a cat and a mouse, but not like the cats and mice in our village. It's a beautiful cat, with a wonderful mouth, warm and sweet and the mouse is not afraid to get into her mouth because she does not eat it, but pets it, keeps it warm and the mouse stays there as long as it wants to; it can even sleep in this cat's mouth, and it can also dance to the most beautiful dance in the world.' She caressed my neck and asked again: 'Do you want my tale?'

'Yes, I do.'

She took my hand and put it on her shirt; I felt her navel under the shirt and my hand trembled. 'Don't be afraid, my mouse.' She pulled her shirt up and my hand touched her soft skin and shivered. Her hand, above mine, moved all over her body, and, then, she moved down, where I felt the softness of a mown lawn and silk put together. 'Look, this is my cat,' she said, holding my hand lightly, as if she feared that the angels would wake.

'What about the mouse?' I asked, slightly lost.

'You have the mouse,' she said. At that instant, her hand slid down my belly, where something had already started to move: something which could have been an angel or the devil itself. With a slight movement, as if I were a feather in wind, the young bride threw me on top of herself. Then, with the other hand, she opened her shirt and took my arm between her two milk-white tits and, as I realised that all the scents of that world were emanating from there, she put the rose bud of her chest in my mouth and began to whisper: 'cat…mouse…cat…mouse…' Enchanted, I started repeating after her 'cat…mouse…cat…mouse…' After a while, our two whispers joined; my mouth and her body joined, my hands with everything under me, and almost at dawn, heaven and earth joined, too.

I fell asleep with that scent of quince which I never wanted to escape. When I opened my eyes at sunrise, she was no longer there. The world was empty.

I heard noise coming from downstairs: doors slamming and stairs cracking, and I got up to leave. As I slowly went down the stairs, I heard someone telling someone across the street: 'Anatolia is dead!'

35

'Get the mule ready and take it to your uncle,' Mother told me one morning. 'He will go to hand over the obligations to the Locality and the horse alone is not enough,' she explained, when a questioning look appeared in my eyes.

'But I won't go with him; we agreed with the King's Son to go for quails.'

'Fine,' Mother said. I looked at her and remorse pierced through my body. She made me feel sorry more than anyone else in the world. From the day when she told the men of the village, 'There is no funeral without a dead man,' and closed the door, both the dead and the funeral had gotten into her soul and bustled in her head every day and every hour. I was born after my maternal uncle disappeared. I had only seen him in some pictures and on the back of the most beautiful among them, MARUBI was written in capital letters. It was the photo of seven soldiers sitting on a big artillery cannon, some on its long muzzle and others on the huge body of the weapon.

'Look, this is your uncle,' Mother would tell me, putting her finger on the one who was sitting first, on the mouth of the cannon. When I heard his whole story, every time Mother spoke to me in that calm and gentle voice of hers, I felt a sting within, as if a shard of broken glass in my chest pricked my heart. But never in my lifetime have I asked Mother about her lost brother; I learned his story through snippets of conversations with others and the sighs coming right from her soul.

He started his own business and became one of the richest men in the village; he would dress in the European style and wear a fedora hat like that of Olloman America. He would come to the village along with his new friends, whom he photographed in the meadows, and he would always carry a bag full of candy, which he distributed to the kids of the village—all of them, from the ones in the first household to the ones in the last. Before the war started, he came with an Italian major, to whom he gifted one of his house's rugs. Together, they uprooted the junipers from the plains of Pladnishta to make a field, where the boys of the village could play ball, in the clothes that the major had brought for them. During the war, he only came once, yet his visit surprised not only the village, but the whole province, for he arrived not by horse, as on other occasions, but by something called motorcycle and which had three wheels. 'Why did you bring this work of the devil, son?' Grandmother Ajnurka had told him.

Nonetheless, in the meantime, all the youth of the village followed the motorcycle, which went around the field in front of the house making a deafening noise. God knows how he had brought it from Prizren, because the paths to our village, to that day, had only seen horses and mules. But it was said that there was a road for cars from Prizren to Dragash and one from there to Buka, and, from there to the village, at times the motorcycle carried him and, at others, he the motorcycle.

'How much does an oke of the farts of Çaush's son cost?' someone asked at the café: precisely in Çaush's café, the most beautiful two-story building in the village, the only one with plaster and windows from the city. While a bandit from the villages across the river, touching his pistol in its holt, had threateningly said: 'How did I not come to find out he was coming and cross his path at Bianec?'

'And you would have shoed the entire gorge with rubber *opinga*', replied one of our villagers who heard him, 'those motorcycle tires were so fit for *opinga*!'

These words circulated all over, as if they were carried with the wind, and reached the ears of Çaushi's son, that is, my uncle. Throughout the war, he didn't come to the village anymore. He stayed in Prizren, where he owned a hotel and a small café. It is said that a beautiful Milica, the sister of a Serbian partisan, also worked in that hotel. When Tito's partisans arrived, my uncle, along with many others, was taken on a night with a torn moon and sent to Zhur's cliffs. He opposed our war, the brother of beautiful Milica was heard saying, when they were tying him with a rope. He wasn't seen ever since. Some said he was in prison, others in exile in Bar; many claimed that he was killed. Hence, some men went to my grandmother's house to express their condolences, but Mother came out to the gate and closed it in their faces.

'There is no funeral without a dead man,' she told them, and they left.

And from that day on, nobody knows if he is dead or alive. Grandmother's household was left with no men. She had no other sons, two of her sons-in-law were in Tirana selling crisps, another had spent the night in Belgrade, while the fourth—my father—was not in the village at all at the time: some said he had been interned to Montenegro, others that he was in Durrës to reopen his confectionery, and others that he was in the villages of Has, or at the foot of Korab, tinning. Grandmother paid some of the village men with gold, and they went to Prizren. One said he met Xhavit Nimani, the other Fadil Hoxha, but all received the same answer: 'We don't know where he is.' When she realised that all of them were deceiving her for her gold, Grandma Ajnurka set out to look for her son on her own. She went to Zhur and Xërxë, to Hoçë and Prizren, found some traces that intermingled with one another, and, eventually, foodless and hopeless, she stood by the Fountain of Prizren. 'Your child leads you to the snake hole and to the enemy door.'

'What are we going to do, Grandma?' asked the grandson she had taken along in that desperate search for her son. She did not speak, as she felt deceived, despised, trampled and mistreated, without shelter or anyone to rely on. As night fell frighteningly over the city, a boy who looked the same age as her grandson approached. The two boys found out that it was the same sort of trouble that united them that gloomy night; the boy from Prizren would also come over there every single day to ask about his father, who had been taken away by the OZNA police and of whom no one had heard anything ever since.

'Come to my house, Mother Dija will welcome you as her own,' the boy said.

'What's your name, son?' Ajnurka asked.

'Bekim.'

'May God and Muhammad bless you! Insha'Allah one day your father comes back and knocks on your door…'

They went to Dije's house and sat around the table of those strangers who were the same as them: just as robbed, just as hopeless, just as deceived, just as imprisoned, just as killed, and just as missing.

It was later learned that beautiful Milica's brother took over the hotel and the cafe, but Milica was no longer seen on the streets of Prizren…

A tear rested on the corner of my eye, and I put my head on Mother's chest to not let her see it. 'Go now. Your uncle is waiting for you,' she said.

'Did everyone hand over their obligations?' I asked Uncle.

'That of the meat. Not of the wool!' he answered.

I didn't get whether he was joking or if he meant it, because I remembered that, in a page of his diary, he had written about a villager of ours who told the debt collectors: 'I have no more wool to hand over, unless you accept my wife's pubic hair.' I would come across these piquant expressions on the pages of the diary quite often. On one page, he had written about the mother of a certain Lemsidin, a villager of ours who went to work on the construction of a factory in Tirana.

'Where is your son?' someone asked her.

'A volunteer, in action,' she replied.

'Volunteer? When did he leave?'

'A week ago, the police took him.'

'We handed our obligations over, of course we did,' Uncle started talking to himself. The plenipotentiary shook the obligation document, yelling his head off: 'Can you read? Then, read it! Here it is written: obligation document, 67 kg of meat, 70 eggs and 2 kg of wool are to be delivered. Obligation documents, buddy, aren't picnic lists that you can go by, in case you feel like it, and not go by in case you don't…' Uncle kept talking to himself rather than me as he loaded the obligation bags…'Not to mention the drudgery of taking them to the Locality…' And he tightened the straps furiously, as if it was my mule's or his horse's fault.

'Why is he called like that?' I asked.

'Who is called like what?' he asked, looking at me confused.

'That plenipotentiary…Majka told me that only God is all-powerful.'

'Majka knows nothing about this world. If God were all-powerful, all this,' he said, patting the sacks with his palm, 'would feed my children, not the *elalem*[65].' I did not understand what the word meant, but I dared not ask, because I saw that a vein had popped on his forehead, and everyone said that this was a sign to not push it.

'Did you mention God?' Uncle continued. 'He threw stones down here that even He cannot lift, he left us wretched. If a mouse happens to fall in our granary, it would break its neck.'

When Uncle left, I did not go up to my grandmother, but immediately entered the small room where he kept his tools and diary. The tools were in their place, but I didn't find the diary where I'd put it a few days ago. I opened the other drawers, turned them upside down, but I couldn't find the bag with the notebooks on which Uncle recorded every passing day. I was stunned and wondered where the notebook could have gone. I wanted to run after Uncle and ask him, but I couldn't possibly do that. I went upstairs and asked Uncle's wife. She yelled at me as if she had seen a ghost.

---

[65] Undefined others

'This is none of your business; go and leave us alone!'

What had happened to that damn diary that made her shout at me like never before? I got upset and started looking for the King's Son. He was also looking for me. We went to the quail basket; it had fallen, but there was neither a quail nor even a sparrow beneath.

'I told you. We should have come yesterday,' the King's Son said, 'our quails were stolen.'

'C'mon, it doesn't matter,' I said, and set off to return. He stood up to set the basket again, but I didn't wait. I hurried with the intention to ask Teacher about the diary. Maybe he knew something.

I waited for him until he finished the lesson.

'Forget about that notebook,' he told me, 'I returned it to your uncle and we burned everything: both the one he wrote and the one you copied. It is a dangerous thing!' he said and turned to go back to class.

'*Pieces of paper, dangerous?*' I thought, enraged. 'Had we had a rifle hidden in the wall, we would have pissed our pants!'

The idea that Teacher did not hear these words calmed me down, not only because I didn't want to say bawdy words in front of him, but also because for fear that he would come back and ask me why I mentioned the rifle. The truth was that three years ago, I had seen Father put a rifle inside the walls of our barn. Indeed, even today after fifty-seven years, it remains there. At times, I have thought of going and getting it, but I haven't, for fear that my wife would repeat those words she had told me countless times: 'Enough with the junk from that village of yours!'

36

I was wandering through all the alleys from where the house of Anatolia could be seen, hoping to see the young daughter-in-law in any of the windows, when Dem Zdrale, a classmate of mine in all four grades of elementary school, and whom I will never forget, as he came barefoot even through the snow and never missed a day of school, called me. 'It's not that I have no *opinga*,' he'd tell us, 'but I do it to keep fit.' His father had been the first goalkeeper of the village team, when the sports association "Kallabak" was established. He was such a good goalkeeper that the song 'Ajdin Zdrale doesn't mess around, he catches the ball in the air' was not sung in vain. Truthfully, his father had saved a penalty right in Shkodra, but his son didn't go around barefoot for exercise. I knew very well that they were broke and had nothing to wear, and when I saw him shivering from the cold, I shivered even more.

'We've caught an eagle,' he told me.

'With a basket?' I asked, because the stolen quail basket occupied my mind, as well.

'A basket? Do you think that eagles are sparrows?'

He gestured to me to enter the small alcove, between the two classes. The first and third grades were taught at the one on the left, whereas the second and the fourth at the one on the right. The only window on the alcove did not illuminate the spot properly, and, under that dim light, all I saw was a cage with wild kittens. I turned to my friend:

'Since when is a wild cat called an eagle?'

But, from half-darkness, he pulled another cage and at that moment I heard the bird's wings hit the cage's slats. I don't know why, but I felt as if the big bird that I had never seen so closely before was looking at me in anger. It continued to flap its wings behind the slats, making a dull sound. Poor eagle, I said to myself. When we were younger, we were scared of the eagles we saw every day above the rocks of our village, because the elders had told us that, with their

160

claws, they grabbed not only lambs but also children; some said that a petite girl from our school, whom everyone called "Fatiçe", was once captured by an eagle, and that's why she didn't grow taller. I had once seen an eagle land on a barley field like an arrow, with my own eyes. And, as I waited for it to get up with some rabbit in its claws, I noticed it had grabbed a snake. It flew very high and dropped it on some cliffs, on which it also landed. To me, it seemed that it was gobbling the pieces of the snake.

'And what are you going to do with them?' I asked Dema. 'The principal's call,' he said and left.

I stayed, listening to the eagle's flapping wings and I don't know what I thought, or maybe I didn't think at all; I had completely forgotten about the quail basket, I had also forgotten that nearby, in another cage, there was a wild cat. Where had they found them? Maybe over there, in Shap. Maybe they were caught by the man who, along with some other bandits, kidnapped that girl from our village and shot at the gates of the Murats to scare people. I thought this because Shap was a steep and rocky place where you could see eagles in flight every day, while the closest house to this area was that of the kidnapped girl, who now was a mature woman with half a dozen kids, and plenty of grandchildren.

'You stare at it on the peaks…' These words, which I had memorised while reading the books Teacher gave me, crossed my mind. I could not bear it any longer and fled. If I had stayed longer, I would have probably cried. My chest was brimming with pain and sadness that day, and I was about to burst, as nobody asked me what the matter was: neither at school, nor on the street, nor at home. Who was going to lose sleep over me? All the time, the sound of the eagle's wings beating the slats resonated in my head, and I was dumbfounded, because at times I imagined them as the white the pages of Uncle's diary, or Teacher's poem…seven Bukojna gates, deserted, the seven. No song had been sung since the girls left. I wondered why I tied the girls to that encaged, exhausted and famished eagle. Back home, I could not eat either.

'Why don't you eat?' Father asked.

'What do eagles feed on?' I asked.

'Oh, you want eagle food!' he joked, but I couldn't even muster a smile.

The eagle appeared in my dream, too, but not in a cage; it was flying in the sky, slashing it into blue pieces with its powerful wings. And the sky started shrinking…it became as small as a sword, and, then, it turned into a cage woven out of clouds and fog, and in which the eagles could no longer be seen. An ugly snow, like stones from the sky, began to fall. I woke up. I didn't wash my face nor did I have anything to eat; I ran to the school. The eagle was still beating its wings behind the cage. In a corner, they had placed some food for her.

'It won't eat,' Dema told me.

When the school principal came, I wanted to leave.

'Did you miss school?' he asked.

Rage and sorrow made me tell him that I was there to visit the eagle, not the school.

'Let her go,' I continued, 'The wild cat is enough; it eats, but the eagle refuses to.' The principal was surprised by these words and stared at me, intrigued.

'Hmm,' he said mockingly. 'Do you think that I am one of those men in the mountains who you taught to put the Koran on stone rather than grass?' Only the mind of a principal like ours, who had eight years of education less than the Teacher from Shkodra, could tell how these two things were related. 'A principal does not need much education; it's enough for him to know how to give orders and even for the order, he does not need much schooling, because the orders come from the Committee,' he would say in the village cafe, where some called him "principal", but most called him "jokester".

'Boy, go to that stingy grandmother of yours, the one with all those lambs, and have one slaughtered for the eagle…and the cat!'

'Feed the cat yourself,' I told him and ran away. Even though I was mad at him, I did as the principal told me to. I went to my grandmother, spun around, and brought wood for her stove from downstairs. She put her head on my lap, and I massaged it lightly with all fingers, without getting bored, until she said: 'Your fingers are magic; only you can relieve my headache.' Ever since her son disappeared, she complained that her head ached incessantly, day and night. 'Only when I get to see him will it be healed.' And so it was. Her headache only ceased when she set out for the hereafter, where she must have met her missing son. I continued to caress her head with my fingers for a little bit more, and when she was breathing softened, I asked her for lamb meat, without telling her why I wanted it.

When I dropped the piece of meat inside the cage, I felt that the eagle was looking at me as fiercely as it had on the first day. She did not touch it at all. Neither that day nor on the following ones. I went every morning with the hope that she would have a bite, but she didn't even look at it. In the meanwhile, she

162

kept flapping her wings…flapping and flapping. One day, I did not see the meat in the cage and rejoiced as never before. '*I'll ask Grandmother for more*,' I thought. Dema stood behind my back.

'We gave it to the cat, because the eagle would not eat it,' he said. I ran away without saying a word. After a few days, the eagle's cage was not there.

'They took it away. Dead.' It was Dema's voice, again. Without turning my head, I glanced at the cat's cage; it stared at me with a savage coldness and, then, continued to munch on the bones she had in its cage.

I didn't go home, but wandered through the meadows that were still under a thin sheath of frost. Some belches of grey mist made the day gloomy. A bunch of finches stopped on a dry cherry branch. I pulled out the slingshot, and shot to scare them without even looking. They flew away, but one fell to the ground. I took it in my hand and felt the warmth of the yellow fluff and a light sigh. I threw the slingshot and ran away, not knowing where to go…Like a flower among rocks, through the stony roofs, the song of young girls—the sisters of those we were still waiting to come for Saint George's—was heard…

Haj mjore Kurto budalla,
Sllushaj shto veli Zejnepa,
Evogo Gjuren iduje,
Zejnepa se omërzilla,
Gjurgjevden go ogrubile,
Teferiç go zamërznale.
Hej, you Kurt, you fool
Lend an ear to what Zejnepa is saying…
Saint George is approaching
And Zejnepa is upset,
As Saint George's is getting ugly,
Joy has been frozen.

The yellow bird's body was cold in my hand, and I didn't know what to do neither with it, nor with myself.

37

The village had become tense, probably because spring was late and so were the girls. The wind that blew cold in the mornings, but even colder by dusk, crashed into the corners of houses, inducing frightful pierces. Fog hid under the roofs of houses and below the windows. The two men, whom the village had sent a few days ago to get permission for the girls to come for Saint George's, were not back yet. The men in the village, the few who had remained—as most had gone all over the country to earn their bread—had begun to beat their wives more often, so much so that, one evening, while chatting at the cafe, they tried to decide how men are divided in this world: into brave and cowards; into those who know how to mow the grass and those who don't; into those who steal and those who aren't thieves; into those who sleep with the same woman until death and those who lust for more; those who drink and those who don't; and in this specific case, into those who would hit their mothers when drunk and those who wouldn't, and into other similar groups. However, most agreed that men were divided into those who beat their wives and those who don't.

'If God asked me whether I want to go to Hell beating my wife, or to Heaven not beating her, I would choose Hell. Cause at least I did not allow the hell on Earth to even fidget!' said one of them, a honker, who was the most passionate in this manly quarrel. I happened to hear parts of this conversation while I was buying salt and kerosene for the house. It reminded me of the quince aroma, of the young daughter-in-law who had left to go to her husband in the mine, and my eyes stung with tears, so I hurried to hear no more of this baneful conversation.

I was startled because in our village—but mostly outside of it—it was said that ours were love marriages. The boys would walk in front of the gates and the girls would give them flowers, and, on Saint George's, they adorned their gates with willows to show how much they loved them; when they came back from exile either abroad or the south of Albania, they brought them frames and threads to embroider and a myriad of other trinkets. Yet, when they got married, they started beating their wives within the very first month. And those few men who did not beat their wives were singled out to be simpletons. This is also how they mocked one of my uncles who, when he saw his wife filling water in the fountain without an overcoat—a black cloth that covered the whole body—instead of kicking her and breaking the jar behind her head, went home, set up the "Singer" sewing machine he had brought from Pristina and started sewing newspapers. And when Grandmother asked him what he was doing, he said: 'I am sewing an overcoat for my wife, as she hasn't got any...'

It was known throughout the village that whenever Xhimo lost a card or dice game in the cafe, he went back home and beat his wife; Çulçle would beat his when the meal was over or under salted; Bubllani when they ran out of grain, shouting why it had finished so fast; Hamdi beat his wife every time guests came to his house and the weirdest was Harun, who beat her even when the cat meowed or the sheep bleated in the yard and woke him from his nap.

'They are all fools; that's why they beat their wives,' Majka would say. 'Fools and fools in *opinga,* at that,' she would add, when someone objected and then enraged left, shouting half in Albanian and half in Gorani: 'Hajt, you shukam vo dashnia.' *I piss in that love of yours!*

'If there was love, they would not kidnap girls, as these brutes are doing,' she told me once. The truth was that, at the time, many girls in our village had been kidnapped.

'We could do nothing to the bandits, who came and kidnapped Rajma with rifles and by force, but these kidnappings, in broad daylight, in the middle of the village?'

Once, when the girls were dancing at a wedding, the one to lead the dance was light-heeled Biljana of beautiful lips. Whenever she shook her handkerchief as if to greet the sky, the boys were buried alive. Then she would turn the handkerchief over her head and the waterfall of her hair seemed even more vibrant, while her body rumbled like the willows on Saint George's. Tuçe Shkoro went straight to the dancing girls and touched Biljana on her shoulder. 'I marked you!' he said, which according to the custom meant that I want you to be my wife and nobody else can touch you. 'Oh, you can have my spring sleep, you vapid bird!' Biljana shouted.

A few weeks later, at another wedding, beautiful Biljana led the dance again and her handkerchief let out a light fragrance of quince. Everyone gazed at her with admiration, either at her handkerchief, with its dreamy sway, at Biljana's sweet eyes, at her feet dressed in socks embroidered with flowers, which seemed to not touch the ground at all, or at her chest blossoming under her vest, with the bronze buttons, which—in my mind's eyes—could pop off any moment, unleashing all the flowers and fragrances of this world. Unexpectedly, two men rushed towards her, grabbed her by her hair and her feet, and dragged her away. The girls who were dancing along her fled away frightened, just like lambs when the wolf kennel attacks. Moreover, Tuçe's friend, who was helping him to kidnap Biljana, was never referred to by his given name; everybody called him "wolf". Although he was still unmarried, he had helped several others to kidnap girls within the village…

Biljana's dreadful screams rattled the stones of the road through which they dragged her; the entire village got up to see what was going on. Biljana was shoved inside a house, as she continued to cry and curse. The post commander with some soldiers and members of the village council went to his door. But Tuçe would not open it.

'You can have her over my dead body!' he shouted from inside.

'You can't hold the girl by force. You are acting against the law,' said the other from outside.

'I'll go to prison willingly, but I won't let Biljana go!'

Even when the commander fired a gun, he did not open the door. Several hours passed like this and nobody could guess what would happen next, when the girl's cries suddenly came to a stop, the door opened, and from the darkness of the house, beautiful Biljana shone at the door, disfigured and without a headscarf as her kidnappers had rendered her.

'Go home,' she told her father and younger sister, who were waiting there with a crowd of curious people, the soldiers and the councillors. 'Go home, I will marry Shkoro,' and went back in.

When the crowd started to disperse, I noticed my aunt coming out of Tuçe's house, her face and clothes all dirty. I came to find out later that she had entered the house from the upper chimney and yelled at Biljana:

'Are you a girl or a bitch? If you are a girl, go out and tell those idiots that you love Shkoro and that you will marry him. Otherwise, you will forever be a bitch, because no one on this Earth will agree to marry a kidnapped girl!'

Biljana shivered to her bones and uttered the only words she could: 'go home.' Then, she remained there, in that unfamiliar hearth that became hers, and where she gave birth to seven children, four of whom survived and three that died either at birth, or when very young. Her screams in labour probably evoked the screams of the day when she was kidnapped. After her last labour, she decided to not give birth anymore, although she had not yet turned 40; the births had not deformed her body and when she walked, the curves of the beautiful dancer appeared. From that day on, for more than thirty years—until she died— she no longer accepted her husband in bed and devoted herself to raising the children that survived.

Biljana shared her life with the man who kidnapped her, but for Ibisha, who was kidnapped from the bed of the one she loved, things went much worse. She loved Vejsel, a quiet and discreet boy, somehow withdrawn. Her family had engaged her to Demir of Klamsha, because his father had sent gold coins from exile. One evening, she left the spinning wheel, with which she was preparing her dowry for Demir, and knocked on Vejsel's door; he took her in without saying a word. As soon as Demir found this out, he and his two cousins went and tore down Vejsel's door, locked him in a room and told him that they would open it only after Demir incarnadined his bed with Ibisha's virginity. But that very same night, Ibisha ran out of the window, and Demir's cousins did not find the bed incarnadined, but Demir himself tied to it.

'How could this happen?' they asked. 'You aren't fit for a woman.'

Ibisha went to her family but they didn't accept her. 'Go back to where you came from!' they told her, without mentioning either Vejsel or Demir's name. She went to Vejsel. At the door, she ran into Demir's two cousins. She was scared to death and bolted, but they called to her and wished her a happy life with Vejsel. They had already opened the door for him; actually, this is why they were there. Ibisha and Vejsel got married, but before they could have children, he fled to a Bosnian town and never returned. After many years of waiting and after the border with Yugoslavia was closed, Ibisha lost all hope that she would see Vejsel again and agreed to marry Zarif Zarbo, the cripple who claimed that he got injured as a partisan. He would boast about his bravery, but everyone had seen him crying from fear when Commander Niazi came to the village to take the young men to war. Some went willingly, others by force.

Zarif had also been involved in a kidnapping issue, years ago. The kidnapped girl refused to be his bride, and nobody had gone in from the chimney to convince her. On the contrary, the council members had torn down the door and asked the girl in front of him:

'Do you want him to be your husband?'

'No, I don't. Take me to Omer Çuça. He is the one I love.'

They took her there, but Omer's mother sent them away, saying:

'I won't have a kidnapped girl as my daughter-in-law; let the one who removed her headscarf from her head enjoy her.'

The girl stayed in the council office for three days; no one came to get her, neither her family, nor that of the boy she loved, to whom she had given a handkerchief embroidered with flowers and who had placed a large willow at her gate.

Once again, the cripple went to take her, but she refused. After three days, they took her to Oreshka; a council member had spoken with a widowed man who had two children, and was happy to marry her.

'She seems to be good both for the bed and the crib,' he said, handing her the two little children—one of them, just a year old—to raise and mother.

'This is how the men of our village are, stupid and narrow-minded and they hit their wives without remorse,' Majka told me, as she finished these girls' stories, which I had heard other times. But hearing them from her was completely different; they became more real, more bizarre. She bundled them in a mystery I never understood the origins of: was it from her eyes, evaporating from old age, or from the hands with which she held the magic spoons and tongs?

'What about our girls? Will they come for Saint George's?' I asked. 'With these men of ours, forget Saint George's, they won't be back even for Eid!'

'What could they do…'

'If it were me in their shoes, I would tell the head of state: either let the girls go, or take dung on your face. For a thousand years, we have celebrated Saint George's with the girls. Spring won't bloom if the beech sprout doesn't.'

38

Majka's words scared me. If someone were to hear her, she wouldn't be taken to the Locality, but to the head of state. Tied and exhausted. Besides Salko, many others had their ears pricked up and eavesdropped on every word one could utter "against". Several men had started eavesdropping on each other; some even went out at night and listened under windows. In the morning, they went to the council, to recount what they had heard: who spoke against the action, against the Locality, against the voting marbles[66], against drudgery or reciprocity, against the obligation documents or the chemical fertiliser. And the severer the report, the more the kilos of obligations the reporter got rid of. The number of eavesdroppers increased particularly on the days—and especially the nights— when, far from the village, in that Tirana where the government resided, there was a conference or a celebration of the kind with military parades. Two months ago, two eavesdroppers who had come out with their handguns had spotted a candlelight that stayed lit too late into the night. They went to see what was going on and spotted a young man making love to his fiancée, still unmarried. It was reported as a "display of foreign ideology", but the issue was not taken too far, because the boy in love passed in front of the council door two or three times with an axe in hand. Someone also reported on a woman singing a song: 'through husk and seeds, two Stalins came up.' Because the council couldn't decide whether the song was "for" or "against", they did not bother with the woman who had sung it. More and more often, an officer would come to the village. He did not meet the men in the cafe or in their houses, but somewhere far from the eyes of the people: sometimes in Rusinica, sometimes in Vlahanica, sometimes in Illojna and sometimes in Mllakojna. Away from the eyes of the people, as a matter of speaking, because True to God, the village always came to learn about

---

[66] Because of the low literacy rates of the time, instead of ballots, votes were cast by throwing marbles into two different boxes, one "for" and one "against"

them: the Security guy met Samet in Rusinica, he met Shuke in Mllakojna, and he met Zemur in Illojna…This is why I was afraid for Majka. She was looked at with suspicion, since the time she sprinkled the gates of the village with blessed water for protection from lice typhus, so that our girls in action would not get sick and die like Zumreta. I was silent as a tomb for every word I heard; I was a mill that would only ground my own flour. But I knew that Majka would not only say these things to me and that one day she could fall prey to Salko or others. My fear intensified the day that she was tied up to be taken to the Locality, the district, or wherever. 'You are ruining our communist morals with foul words!' Salko had accused her.

It had been a few days since two families of our village started to quarrel, and the issue had gone as far as men fighting, women scratching and pulling each other's hair, and the grabbing of axes and slashes by the most heated of both families. It was the case of a meadow sale. Two years after the sale, the seller came to the village after having gathered the meadow money through some small trades in Tirana, threw it to the buyer, and said:

'Give me the meadow back.'

'The meadow was sold. You traded with my money and now here you come, two years later, and ask for my meadow. Are you out of your mind?'

'I may or may not be. I want the meadow!' Aware that the other would not give in back, he brought up the beech trees that were found in the middle of the meadow.

'You can have the meadow, but I did not sell the beeches!'

The following day, he cut down two beeches and took them home. Then, the other family also drew their axes, not to cut down beeches but heads. Men assembled to reconcile them, but the conflict had no end in sight. 'I want my beeches!' the first shouted. 'When you sold me the meadow, you sold it along with the beeches!' the other replied. For a week or two, the men tried to mediate this quarrel, the commander of the post office and the head of the Locality also got involved, but the dispute would not end. When Majka heard that, the sons of the two families had been about to maim each other with axes, she got dressed and left for the council. Her cane knocked on the cobblestones of the road, as if it was counting down someone's days, but whose, it was not known. I followed her, even though some of my peers made fun of me, saying that I had become the grumpy old woman's pet. She didn't find anyone in the council. Everyone had gathered in the cafe beating their brains out over the men who would be killed over a meadow.

Many were the men from our village that had been killed. For eight pairs of *opingas*, or even a horse. Our mountain shepherd, Bajram Luli, was killed, to steal our sheep. A young man had been murdered a few days after his wedding, to rob him of his watch with a golden chain. Yet, all these had been committed by outsiders. But now murder was boiling inside the village, among ourselves. When Majka entered the cafe, nobody noticed her, but she hit the floor with her centennial stick and all the men went quiet.

'What does this hag, forgotten by death, want in the men's cafe?' Salko said.

'Where are those two?'

In the opposite corners of the café, the two men who had been quarrelling over the meadow straightened up.

'You who sold the meadow, tell me, what is this called?' she asked, placing her hand below her belly, between her two legs. 'Speak! You are brave enough to fetch the axe to kill but you are afraid of saying a word, you freckleface!'

Some of the men had lowered their heads, others grinned as if caught in guilt.

'Then, you speak, Olloman of America, as you are the eldest and you are no longer ashamed of these words. Tell me, what is the name of this thing of mine, and give me no substitutes, but the name as it is!' she said, addressing him, without removing her hand from below her belly. Olloman was gloomy and uncomfortable, but, when Majka lifted her cane and hit the floor and the ceiling, he murmured: 'It's a cunt.'

'What about that black thing around it?'

'Cunt hair…'

'Did you hear that?' she asked the one who had sold the meadow. 'When you sell the cunt, ask for its hair no more!'

She left. The men were speechless; nobody moved. The silence, which lasted several minutes, was broken by Salko.

'Did you hear that? How can these words be said in front of the council and in front of all these men?' he shouted, looking at both sides. 'These words fall against the communist morality. I will inform the Locality police.' His voice was even more solemn when he noticed that nobody was paying him any attention.

'Sit on that ass of yours, Stalin, you and all the morals you are showing us,' Uncle exclaimed.

The men started to leave one after the other; only the two quarrelling over the meadow stayed. Uncle offered both a cup of tea, and the three sat down at a table. I ran to reach Majka, who, holding onto her ancient cane, was talking with the stones of the village.

39

Two days later, I cursed myself a thousand times for the evil I foresaw; I thought I was the instigator of what happened to Majka. Early in the morning, the dogs were heard barking and Mother asked: 'Who came?' Not who came to our house, but who came to the village, because all breeds and kinds of barks we had in the Upper Neighbourhood could be heard. She went out to the porch from where she came back worried.

'The blacks have come to Majka,' she said, and tried to calm down by coaxing the fire, the wood in which would stubbornly refuse to burn.

I got up immediately and left. Mother did not say a word, because she sympathised with my affection for Majka, which started the day—or even before—she crossed Father's path and shouted: 'What is this ungodliness you are doing? Is this how you beat up the sprout of God in the middle of the road?' She was aware that I spent more time with Majka than I did with my two grandmothers put together.

The Locality police were knocking on Majka's door fiercely.

'What have you done, you mischievous woman who brings us all the way from the city and makes us cross Qafa e Gjarprit[67], just because you can't keep that mouth of yours shut? You can't keep your mouth shut, nor your ass still,' one of the police officers told her as soon as she opened the door. 'Stalin's basement and the Locality cellars didn't suffice; now you are being summoned to the City Command!' the policeman continued, while pulling a small rope from the bag.

'Will you tie me up?' she asked. The cop seemed to have been shaken from sleep.

'God forbid!' he said, looking at the other who was silent and motionless. 'And be cursed by jinn? No, no, I won't tie you; I believe he won't spy on me.

---

[67] Serpent's Pass

Will you?' he added looking at his colleague. 'It is shameful to tie a ninety-year-old woman.'

'She is three hundred,' I said.

'And you? What are you doing here, and where did you come up with the three hundred years?'

'Go home,' the police officer threatened me.

'This is my house,' I replied, trying to deepen my voice.

'Good, good' Majka said, 'I appreciate it because I would feel ashamed to go around the village all tied up.' As if she knew what would happen beforehand, she was already dressed and looked ready for the journey.

'How long do those in the city keep one?' she asked. 'How much food should I take with me?' The two cops shrugged.

'You have stepped into a big swamp, I don't know,' the police officer who seemed to be the other's chief said.

'Big, with thorns and thistles,' Majka said.

'Don't drag us into this,' he told her.

'There are also plenty of mice in this swamp,' said Majka, 'mice from our village, who come every night to tell you and that state of yours what we eat, when we sneeze, when our ears itch, how many spoons we've got...' She went in, counting all of what the mice did and came out quickly with a bag of food.

'Let's go, chief!' she said to the first cop. When I saw them set off on foot, that legendary old woman walking between two police officers—one ahead and the other behind—I was horrified. Would you take her there on foot?

'We do all our tasks on foot,' said the younger one, who, until that moment, had not uttered a word. I ran to the stable, put the saddle on the mule, took the fodder bag, and shouted to Mother:

'I'll accompany Majka. They're taking her to the city.'

Many people had come out to the street and thresholds; they chatted with one another, as they kept looking at the path Majka and the two policemen had just passed. Many of those who had just heard the news, but did not yet know the whole truth, alarmed and astonished, wanted to learn more, while many of the women started weeping.

'Did they kidnap her? Where did they take her?' called a stammering woman. 'Who took the poor thing?'

'Was some girl kidnapped again?'

'There are no girls left in the village, they are now taking old women!'

The people were loud, but I could not understand anything from the crap that was being said all over the street. The dogs came out of their kennels and started barking. Only the words of a woman at the gate of the Xhelils were etched in my mind:

'O God, how unguarded you have left us! Is that how an old woman should be treated?' I felt my blood boil. No, I'm not leaving her alone. I won't leave Majka alone, even if these two policemen with rifles on their shoulders and guns strapped to their belts were to take her to the end of the world! I hurried to reach them. Even outside the village, they marched the same way, in a row: Majka in the middle, one of the cops in front and the other behind her. I hurried the mule and when I reached them, I told Majka to get on the mule.

'Don't cause trouble, boy!' the younger cop told me. But the other one helped Majka get on the saddle.

'We are not going against the orders,' he told the other.

'They told us to take her to the city; they did not say anything else: tied or untied, riding or on foot, with or without a headscarf.' The other shook his head.

'What about you?' he asked me, 'did you take permission at home?'

'Good deeds do not need permission,' I replied.

Although I was curious to know whether their eyes had whites or were completely brown, like those of the bear, I did not want to look into them.

As we were crossing the last mountain meadows of our village, we heard someone shouting from behind. I turned my head and saw men and women rushing towards us; when I counted them for the first time, I got ten, the second time, I got eleven. In front, and walking faster than everybody else, was Teacher.

'What is this shameful thing you are up to?' he shouted, when he approached us. The two policemen stepped forward.

'Mind your own business,' said the first.

'Let us perform the state's duty,' said the other in a thick voice.

'What state is this that seizes old women in broad daylight?'

'Would it be better if we took you?' they replied threateningly.

'Take me! Take me now!' cried Teacher. 'Where are your handcuffs?'

'We have rope, not handcuffs.'

'Tie me with whatever you want, with handcuffs, with rope, with chains. Whatever! And take me to Hell, if you want. But leave this old woman here, where God left her.'

Two or three men, who had come with him, tried to calm him down. Others, men and women, stood dumbfounded and did not know what to say; some had turned red, others yellow, some had no blood on their faces, but the shadow of fear darkened the eyes of them all.

'I won't let you take Majka!' Teacher did not give in and grabbed the mule by its bridle. Majka was trembling on top of the saddle, trembling at something much stronger than fear, as she looked at Teacher not as an ordinary man, who taught kids the multiplication table, but as an outlandish being, who came from the end of the world and who had run through the streets of the village, dragging along those terrified people.

'Let us pass!' the younger cop shouted, but did not move.

'Do not call trouble upon yourself, Teacher,' said the other, the chief. 'Stay where you found shelter by night, as you haven't come from Shkodra to lay the law…'

'It is you who is laying the law, not the Teacher.' Finally, one of the villagers intervened.

'You are laying it with rope and handcuffs,' said another, even more furiously. One of the women could not restrain her anger anymore:

'Let Majka go! Otherwise, I'll gather all the women of the village and we will come with you. Put us all in prison! Where has it been seen that one's mouth is covered with thorns for a single word that is spoken!'

The policemen would not speak anymore. The younger one approached and shoved Teacher, but he did not let go of the mule's bridle; on the contrary, he pulled it to turn the animal. Then, a red vein became visible on the cop's forehead, his expression darkened, and he rushed towards Teacher, seized the bridle and hit him in the chest with it to take hold of the mule, along the old woman riding on it. My poor mule, quiet as it was, watched undisturbed as those two men argued over the bridle and the old woman atop, and who, after all, was not a weight that strained it. The young police officer pushed him even harder and pulled the bridle so fast that Teacher wobbled and would have fallen had those nearby not held him. Two of the men rushed and took the bridle from the cop's hand. Left with no other choice, he withdrew.

'Do as you please, but you will be held accountable.'

'This, only this troublemaker from Shkodra, will be held accountable', the older policeman said, 'and not only for what happened today.'

He grabbed the other cop by the sleeve and they went away; the younger one turned his head back two or three times, while the chief rushed without looking back. We also headed back without speaking. Only Majka broke the silence.

'This is always the case with trouble; it crosses your path midway and right on the day you expect it the least...' I was looking at her in amazement, and it seemed to me that, that morning, she has grown a hundred years older...

40

Throughout the day, it seemed as if the village had closed its gates; there was almost nobody to be seen in the streets, and even those who were out seemed to keep to themselves. I felt the fear that had embraced the whole village as soon as I entered the house and heard Mother talking loudly to herself:

'What will they do to the poor Teacher?' I felt deafened and could not hear a word, as if everyone had become dumb, as if their tongues had been cut off, like the tongue of Majka's great grandfather, who supposedly was everyone's great-grandfather. Only when the tranquillity of the forest of that late April night began to groan over the village, Craple's call, as if it were coming from a dark well, was heard: 'Aye people, villagers…All those who beat the cops should present themselves at the organisation's basement Aye people, villagers Ayee…Ayeeee…' It had been a while since Craple headed in the direction of the Lower Neighbourhood, but his voice, which sounded like the creaking of an abandoned gate, echoed in my ears, and, at times, it felt as if he was not calling from the main street of the village, but as if his voice came straight from my guts.

The room was spinning. I ran outside, but I started vomiting before even having reached the porch of my house. Mother came right away, held my forehead with both hands, and, when I finally calmed down, she pulled me by the arms and put me to bed. 'You'll go nowhere! You have no business in the basement!' For the first time, I heard Mother speak in a different tone; for the first time, I heard her mention the "basement" and I smiled. I knew that when it came to her brother's disappearance, she believed it had happened somewhere, in some "basement".

The following day, before dawn, I went to Teacher. He seemed very distracted, so I didn't ask him what had happened the previous night in the basement, although I was curious to know what had been said, who had participated in the meeting, whether there were any delegates, and everything else related to Majka's case. But it seemed like Teacher did not want to be bothered; I had never seen him so distant, even though we were in a four by four meter room, where there was nothing but a bed, a closet, a table and a crooked chair. He was rummaging through the books, flipping through their pages one by one and whatever he found there—pieces of paper, leaflets, and postcards—was either put on the table or in the closet. On a sheet from a lab notebook, I saw an untitled poem; it was in Teacher's handwriting, which I recognised immediately. But on it, there was no signature, no date, nor the place where it had been written. I took it in my hand and started reading it:

Bora po bie si blozë
Ahet po digjen n'errësirë,
Lloha e jugës na kalb,
Ah, lulet po thahen pa mbirë!
Dua te vdes, por s'më lënë,
A mundem ta ngrys këtë jetë?
'Përpara, përpara marshojmë!'
E shpirti na vyshket përditë.
Ra morti, por ne nuk u pamë,
Vallë, kush m'i grabiti dhe sytë?
E qorrazi honeve ramë,
Të bijtë e një mjegulle t'hirtë.
E nisem tani n'botën tjetër…
Ndal! Kush kalon? Gërvima e vjetër! [68]

Snow falling like soot
Beeches burning in the dark,
The south wind rotting us,
Flowers drying without sprouting!
I want to die, but they won't let me,
Can I end this life?
'Forward, forward we march!'
And our souls wither every day.
Death befell, but we saw each other not.

---

[68] It's an acrostic poem, the reading of the first letters of each line is "Ballade per veten", that is "Ballad to myself"

Who, I wonder, also robbed my eyes?
And blindly fell in abysses,
We, the sons of a dim fog.
I'm leaving for the hereafter…
Stop! Who goes there? The old yelp!

I was lost in those lines; everything seemed to be a riddle, and I did not notice that Teacher was staring at me with a book in hand, frozen. I left the piece of paper on the table and did not dare to look up; reading those lines was so strange to me:…snow falling like soot…death befell, but we saw each other not…we, the sons of a dim fog…they pulsed on my temples like the simultaneous rolls and grinds of a hundred mills. Teacher collected some more pieces of paper, put them in an envelope and gave them to me.

'Take them to your uncle, right now!' he commanded. 'Let him keep them in his diary, as relics from the Teacher.'

'He no longer keeps the diary,' I said and explained to him that I had searched everywhere, but had not found it.

'Let him start one anew,' laughed Teacher. 'Go now,' he told me, 'go, as they are about to come…'

They…who? They, they…In my village, when someone was possessed by demons or jinn, we said *"they"* got to him; we were afraid of mentioning *them*, because mentioning their names could make *them* haunt us, too.

Suddenly, someone knocked on the door as if they were churning milk. I instinctively put the papers Teacher gave me under my vest. Two policemen and Salko, along with two others, got in. The lips of one of the strangers were as dry as a walnut's shell.

'Go home and don't worry, the school will surely open next fall,' Teacher told me.

'What are you doing here?' Salko addressed me.

'I came to ask about the school.'

'He may be a teacher; but it is us who opens the schools. And it is not certain if he will be a teacher anymore…'

I left without saying a word; at that point, I felt as if I had forgotten how to speak. I clasped the papers under my vest and went home. Mother was worried I would vomit again and put her hand on my forehead. 'No, I'm ok,' I said. Then, I pleaded and begged her to show me the place where Father hid the gold.

'Who told you?' Mother asked me. I shrugged.

'We have no gold,' Mother said. I was perplexed and didn't know what to do with the "gold" I had hidden under my vest.

41

Teacher was made to put all books in a sack and carry them to the basement on his back. Two of his students who happened to see the scene, hurried to carry the sack.

'I saw a tear rolling down his cheek,' one of them told me. The next day, a dozen unknown men came to the village: two police chiefs, a committee secretary, two or three who were called propagandists—I didn't know what their job was—some police officers and the strangest among them was the one they called "the writer". 'He will be rummaging through the Teacher's letters and books,' they said of him. During the day, they summoned Teacher and at night, they went to the houses of the villagers to rest.

This was always the case when people sent by the state came; they passed the night in our houses, following an order set by the council. But this time, there was no order; in groups of two, the delegates went to the houses of the villagers who were with Teacher on the day Majka was rescued from the police. Yet, none of them went to Majka's house, nor did they ask her about that event; they must have known the answer. From the overnight stays of the delegates, versions of the event started to come out and to slide through the mud of the village. They'd say that Teacher had hit the police officer; that he had said 'what a shitty state this is, taking hold of old women in the middle of the day'; that 'this is the rule of handcuffs and rope'; that 'life has turned into hell', etc., etc. Every passing day, two policemen picked up someone from the village and took him to the Locality or district to interrogate. One, whose brother had fled abroad, had taken some clothes and carpets from his sibling's house. All these goods were loaded on his back and he was sent to the Locality where he was held for three hours. From there, he was sent to the district—a nine hour walk away—still carrying the goods of his brother's house. The following day, he was returned to the village—the goods still on his back—and ordered to hand everything over to the council through an official document. Another day, they took two men to deliver their obligations to the Locality, not by horse or mule, but on their backs. On the way, the cops would constantly make fun of one of them: 'is your wife's hair tiring you?' This because, two months ago, when they went to his house to take his obligation on wool, he had told them: 'I have not a bit more; the only thing left is my wife's pubic hair, but I don't think you want it, because you only want white wool.' A woman was summoned to be interrogated about a dream she was said to have recounted to some women while fetching water from the village fountain. I saw, she had explained, Mullah Isuf, and he was upset. Tell my nephew to read and learn from the books I left him and not those brochures for Stalin's truck drivers.

'Who told you this dream?' they asked.

'I had it myself…I have also had other dreams. In a dream, I saw you, Stalin, mowing the grass in our meadows beyond the soft belt. You were with the post captain. I saw you…'

Her last dream made Salko put an abrupt end to the conversation, saying: 'Let her dream with her eyes open; we have work to do.' The next day, they confiscated all the books of Mullah Isuf, and, to this day, no one knows where they took them. They must have burned them.

When the police took the third man, the entire village went out to look. They had loaded two real rifles and a toy gun on his back. He was accompanied not by two, but by four police officers. It was Samul of the Isaac neighbourhood. It was said that his real name was Samuil, like that of one of his ancestors, but nobody in the village could twist their tongue to properly pronounce that "uil", so they called him Samul. 'He has made the rifles himself,' said some, looking astounded at the weapons, one of which had a white, freshly skimmed and unpainted wax butt. 'He has really made it himself, at least the new one,' people said. Everyone knew that he collected old rifles, thrown here and there since the last war, even those that were not used as anything other than gate latches. He had not forgotten the craft of his ancestors of his neighbourhood, and, out of ten or twelve old rifles, he had crafted the two he had on his back. He had certainly made the toy rifle for one of his children to play "pretend war". Once, when he and my maternal uncle's son went shooting at Përroi i Shurdhër[69], they made me stand guard at Guri i Çekiçit[70] and alert them in case anyone approached. The man with his exiled brother's belongings and the man with wool obligations

---

[69] The Deaf Brook

[70] The Stone Maul

came back home, while the "man who crafted rifles" did not. 'They put him in jail.' This news shook the village. I had begun to tremble for the fate of Teacher, who seemed to have been pulled into mist. And it seemed that that fog was now also pulling me in.

42

It had been days that the whirlpool of a fear never known before was leading the village with no girls into a meaningless clash and to a gloom, in which no one could see the other, in which they could hear but did not understand each other, in which they rarely had coffee together and did not ask 'how did you sleep last night?' in the morning, for fear of the answer and the suspicion embodied in every word. In short, the whole village was mired in the fog of confusion and misunderstanding. Almost nobody, not even his students, spoke to Teacher. But some elderly women were seen wiping their tears by their houses, when they saw him going to school every morning. The people were so disoriented that when the village envoys—sent to ask permission for the girls to spend Saint George's at home—returned, they looked at the two startled, as if receiving news of something distant and half-forgotten.

'We have started a second life,' said Majka, when they informed her that her granddaughter would not come for Saint George's. 'A second life that is no longer solely in the hands of God…,' and she closed the door, something she had never done in three hundred years: send someone away without inviting him in for a coffee, for a glass of buttermilk when she had no coffee, or for a peeled quince or chestnuts, in case she didn't have even any buttermilk left.

The two men froze. 'What has happened to them?' My two grandmothers would go to Majka almost every day and stay there for hours, even though they didn't have particularly close relations as in laws. Seemingly, that old house, left desolate for days, and the shared sorrow and fear united them. Majka's real age was quite noticeable those days, and she looked as if she were my two grandmothers' mother. And when she talked to them about things only she knew, she even looked like their grandmother.

'Evil has always been behind us; its food ready in the bag. We fled and it followed…The first persecution was that of our Bogomil ancestors. Then came the time of the second persecution, when they set the priest on fire, to roast him alive like a lamb! During the third one, they burned down the Mosque of Sinan Pasha! After the three days of the Hour[71], the fourth is even worse. When it comes, there will be no stone left unturned...'

She'd say these words almost in a whisper and wait for the Hour to knock on her door.

But Majka was not summoned anywhere, after the day we saved her from the cops. The rest of us, all who were there—men and women, and eventually me—were dragged into the basement to be interrogated. My heart skipped a beat, my eyes glazed over and my mouth went dry, when I was taken there, and, in front of me, appeared Sergeant Hate, who had taken another name: Hate the investigator.

Investigator...Investigator...I knew I should no longer ask Teacher about these new words, but I had no one to ask and my chest burned with desire to learn what this title that had summoned me to the basement was.

'It means sleep killer!' Teacher told me. 'And it comes from the ancient Indian language,' he joked.

But when I faced Hate, my knees started to knock, as they had on the first day I had entered the basement, bleeding. He was the same short man, with dark hair cut short and small eyes that seemed to have been dyed in alder water. From sergeant to investigator, only two elements about him had changed: he no longer wore military clothes and, instead of a gun, he had a chain in hand and he swung it to the right when he asked questions and to the left when one answered. I was more scared when investigator Hate came to Grandma's house with two cops, called Uncle, and commanded:

'Bring me the diary!'

'I don't have it, I burned it a year ago,' Uncle said briefly and hardly answered any other questions.

'Why don't you speak?' insisted the other.

'Because I feel like the master of what has not yet come out of my mouth and the slave of what has. This is why you have come to bind me with words, isn't it, investigator Hate?'

The other shook his head instead of swinging his chain.

'Have you wised up?' Hate asked him.

---

[71] Apocalypse

186

'No other way around it. You just make us wise up,' Uncle told him, 'and now we know that when burned by milk, you blow on cold water,' he added, enraged and frustrated.

Luckily, I was not asked about the letters, but only about the conversations I had with Teacher.

'Why would you go there so often, you've finished school,' he said during one of the basement interrogations.

'No, I haven't,' I responded, shaking, 'I have only finished grade four. Teacher has told me that there are other schools, middle school, high school, university which is a great school, the greatest, I guess. This is why I would visit Teacher. He knows these things well, so I'd go to him and not to Ziko Roçka[72].'

'Who do you think you're making a fool of, you mischievous thing?' He shouted right in my nose and I smelled the heavy odour of pickled onions and cabbage. 'What is this *roçka* of yours?'

'Ziko Roçka,' I said, and he was about to slap me in the face, but, to my surprise, Salko held his hand.

'It's the name and surname of a villager; just as the boy said it.'

'You even have *Roçka* as a name? How could these heinous events possibly not happen here?' He wanted to know more about Ziko, and because Stalin kept serious, he turned to me:

'Do you know anything about him?'

'I do,' I answered.

'C'mon, tell us!'

'I once heard that his cat ate the eggs in the egg-roost. It is rare for cats to do this; they pierce the egg with their front teeth and then drink it…So he threw it on the roof, but nothing happened. The cat used its claws and did not fall down. When it ate the eggs again, he took four walnut halves, removed the kernels and filled them with beeswax. He put them on the cat like *opinga,* and, when he threw it on the roof again, the cat could no longer hold on and fell on the cobblestones and broke its neck.'

'Interesting guy, this Roçka of yours…What does he do with chickens?'

'I don't know about his chickens, but I've heard the rooster's story. His neighbour's rooster crowed very early, and this infuriated Ziko.

He told his neighbour to get rid of it because it woke him up at midnight, but he swore at him saying that he would not stop the rooster's song for Roçka's

---

[72] The term is also a euphemism for male genitals

sleep. One day, Ziko caught the rooster and dunked his ass in oil; the rooster tried hard but it could not make a sound; the song blew out of his butt. A day or two later, its owner slaughtered the rooster, because he only kept it for its song…'

I almost forgot who I was talking to, but he reminded me himself:

'And the Teacher, does he sing? Has he recited you poems?'

From the way he was looking at me, I realised that the "sleep killer" had tried to lull me with Ziko Roçka's stories, just to come to that jarring question. I felt as if there was no ground beneath my feet: no floor, no compacted mud. I felt a thick, dark grey fog was about to swallow me, and I could no longer see Hate the investigator before my eyes.

'Which poems did he recite to you?'

I came out of the fog drenched in sweat.

'Bagëti e Bujqësi[73],' I said, incapable of recognising my own voice.

'You seem to need the "cat treatment", too, you cricket,' he said ironically. 'We'll use it, we will! And your feet won't stand neither on the roof nor the tiles, nor the sky, nor the ground! Bring him to the city tomorrow,' he ordered the two basement cops.

---

[73] A very famous poem written by the Albanian Renaissance Movement thinker and writer Naim Frasheri and which was part of the official educational program even during the Communist regime.

43

Nine hours on the road, without exchanging a single word. To this day, I don't know why he did not say anything to me on the way to hell. Did he not want to upset me because of the fevers that would strike me fairly often, at the time; was he confident that I'd say what should be said when the investigators interrogated me, as I had done in the village and Locality; or was he afraid that providing me with advice would also pull him in the whirlpool I had thrown myself into? He didn't make a sound; he walked in front of me, while I, riding on the mule, stared at Father's shoulders. He seemed more crooked than ever.

How long had I dreamed of this trip to the city—to the school there—especially after Father's words that he would even sell his pillow, if need be, just to send me to school. Maybe it was this promise of his that made my first trip to the city even more difficult. I had lost everything I had kept in the hearth of my childhood dreams; I didn't even care that, for the first time, I would be seeing cars, the buses which went to Tirana or Shkodra, the cinema, the Committee with the balcony where two-three years ago Enver Hoxha came out to greet the people and to deliver a speech. I had only one wish: to be done with this nightmare of an investigation and beg Father to go to the market for a pomegranate; if not a large one, at least two or three small ones, their seeds red like rubies.

A couple of years ago, when all the children of the village contracted measles and were filled with blotchy patches, I too rubbed shoulders with death; it seemed as if it was sitting right there, taking my breath away. I had the same dream several times; there was a long rope that I twisted and twisted, and the moment I tried to tie the knot to hang it in a braid, it would loosen up and, all over again, I would start twisting that damned rope, which would never obey. Twist and groan…twist and groan…twist and groan.

I felt a cold hand on my forehead and, realising that it was not the wet cloth Mother put, I opened my eyes. I saw that it was Father, who had returned from a long journey, which had lasted several weeks or months; I could not count the days while shivering with fever. 'Are you any better?' I tried to answer with my eyelids, but they were heavy as bullets. When I opened my eyes again, Father offered me three or four red seeds; he put them in my mouth and, for the first time, I tasted the flavour I would never forget. That strange fruit with hundreds of rubies lined up in its chambers would also be ingrained in my imagination. 'What is it?'

'Pomegranate,' Father said. Although all the children who contracted measles had been taken to Guri i Çekiçit, made to drink donkey milk and go through an iron circle wrapped in burning cloths soaked in kerosene; I always believed that it was neither the circle of fire, nor kerosene, nor donkey's milk to have healed me, but those heavenly-flavoured seeds.

I don't know why, even on that day, when we were going to the city, to the investigator, without measles and without a fever, without a braided and loosened rope, I had only one wish, to put two or three pomegranate seeds in my mouth. I did not say this to Father for fear that I would wake the lion and he would shout: 'Your highness desires pomegranate too, huh?' When we reached Qafa e Gjarprit and the descent began, we exchanged places with one another; he rode on the mule, and I walked. I was relieved because, on the saddle, I felt guilty and wicked.

44

They took me through a corridor painted in the colour of rotten grass in a rainy and foggy autumn, and then to an office with a high ceiling, on top of which hung a lamp tied with a chain like the one investigator Hate swung. Yet, this one was much thicker. Meanwhile, Hate had put his chain in the pocket and looked at me threateningly, but spoke not. The questions were asked by another man, slightly older, who spoke faster than the "sleep killer" of our village. As soon as he started, I noticed that he was a toothless sour being. He asked me the same questions, with the difference that he repeated each five or six times and, without being able to finish my words, almost shouting, he urged: 'Answer quickly! Right away! Quickly! Immediately!' As if in the measles daze, I kept whispering 'Bagëti e Bujqësi…bagëti e bujqësi…' and it seemed to me that after each question, he dunked me in a creek of icy water. All of a sudden, he struck me with a question I had never heard before:

'And did the Teacher listen to the Voice of America?'

I was dumbfounded and did not understand what he meant. 'What, what?' I stammered.

'The radio has not reached the village yet,' investigator Hate intervened. 'There is no electricity.'

'Aha!' the other said. 'He listened to it in the city, at his mistress.'

At one point, when they both lit cigarettes and were not dealing with me, I told them that, on that day, Teacher neither said 'shitty state' nor 'hell of a state,' and that someone had slandered.

'Who asked you?' Hate scolded me.

'*Bizarre*,' I thought, '*they claim that they defend the state but accept unsaid words as truth; so, they are the ones who make the state both shitty and hellish!*'

After two days, I could no longer make out where I was and I talked to myself, often repeating: 'Dear Mother, where are you? Hold my hand or this abyss will swallow me. Oh Mother!'

When I came out, I found Father on the sidewalk in front of the Station, leaning against a poplar tree, his head in his hands. It seemed as if he had stayed there, without food or sleep, for a whole century. We crossed Drin, to where one of his brothers who worked in the city lived. When I stepped foot on the bridge, I felt it shaking, but, then, I realised that the tremors were in my soul, as the bridge linked the two shores between life and death. It had always been this way. Under the bridge, dressed in white, the Dervish of Kolsh had gotten into the water and kept calling, his hands open to the sky. He no longer shouted: 'This bridge is cursed,' but something else. Some bad omen, just for me. This is how it seemed to me: This boy is cursed, cursed…cursed! Unexpectedly, it seemed as if the river began to flow backwards, as if the Dervish rose above the water and began to fly with open arms towards the sky…

Father held my hand tighter. 'Are you dizzy?' I stopped looking at it, but for the longest of times, the river remained in my imagination with its waters rushing backwards and the Dervish flying towards the sky. 'Who will save me from this curse that has gripped me?' The Dervish's words clashed with the foam of Drini i Zi.

We returned to the village on the first day of Saint George's, the day of the Gora flowers. We would get up early in the morning and go to the meadows above Orgosta; only there did mountain flowers bloom so early—yellow flowers with tassels smelling of spring. We would split a hazelnut branch down the middle, fill it with Gora flowers, tie it with strings—so that the flowers would not fall—and come back singing and laughing loudly. It felt like we were bringing the spring to the village.

When I got home, I learned that none of the village children had gone to pick flowers on that day. As if in a dream, I thought they had been waiting for me, but then I heard someone say that it was such a foggy day that the children were scared to go. The next day—called the day of herbs—there was no girl left in the village to go out into the fields and gardens to gather the first herbs and plants of spring, especially the wild squash, which was thought to ward off the diseases and maladies of cows. On the third day, no young man went to cut the largest and most beautiful willow to put on the gate of his beloved. And on the fourth day, May 6, nobody dressed up in Saint George's clothes, not even Salko. To all of us, it seemed that it would be unfair to the girls who had not been allowed to come—even for two days—and go back again. Also, there were no visitors from other cities for Saint George's, as had always been the case. God had told the

Gorani: I give you a stone, and the stones of your village will gather you from all over. Even if you go to the moon, you will return to your stones. When the border was open, the people of our village would come on Saint George's from Prizren and Mostar, from Tirana and Istanbul, from Gevgelija in Macedonia, from Soluna in Greece and from Bucharest in Romania. They all came, rejoiced, and when they returned to their job in exile, on the streets of the village, they left the unquenchable longing and the saying of the gone 'vizier for three days, *rezil*[74] for the year!' But it was only on that Saint George's we came to realise that it was not the stones of God that called people, but the songs of the soul, the gurgling from the spout of the girls' lips that shone like pomegranate seeds.

The village seemed to be struck by a calamity.

But the true calamity happened in the evening. Seven police officers came and took Teacher away. They tied both his legs and hands with rope, while the white collar of his shirt looked like a piece of cloud broken off the sky, about to fall into abyss…

I didn't know where to go and my tears fell on Majka's lap like hail. She put her hand—just skin and bone—on my hair, and spoke to herself: 'We must have been born of the witches of heaven, as we brought sorrow to the earth…Instead of diapers, they wrapped us in fog…and as shrouds, we will have fog…Chilam…Balam…Chumayel.'[75]

---

[74] Disgraced

[75] The reference is obviously to the Books of Chilam Balam of Chumayel, that Maya miscellanies that shed light on the Yucatec-Maya spiritual life. In the Gorani tradition, it is the curse of the Plague.

45

I was gripped by fear, and I ran home breathless. I removed the hidden stone ad my heart calmed down; no one had touched the papers Teacher gave me…I went into the scullery where we kept the jars and shakes with pickles and pears in water, hid in a corner among them and started to look at the papers; besides the poem that I read in his room, there were also others. I saw some letters that someone, whom I did not know, sent to him sometimes from Shkodra and sometimes from Kukës. Then my eyes caught a yellowed piece of paper with the caption: 'Voice of America on Gora and the Gorani.' Unlike other times, numbness climbed from my feet all the way to my head; I stood like that, with my ears pricked up in fear, but there was no sound other than that of the fear lingering within me.

'So this is why the investigators asked me about this Voice of America.'

And I still didn't know what it was, because those three or four people I had asked had not answered me at all. Instead, they had looked at me as if I were the devil incarnate, or as if I had contracted not just lice typhus, but black cholera. And why did Teacher need these details on our province? On another piece of paper, I read a note from a historian, taken from the 'Ottoman Records,' as Teacher had written down. It said that in 1571, Bukojna had 41 houses, paid 3040 aspers in taxes and had 9 bachelors. In 1592, it's not known how many houses were left and whether or not there were bachelors and whether it paid taxes or not. In 1571, Bukojna was under the command of Mustafa, Colonel of the Dukagjini Sandzak, while, in 1591, it was under the command of Sulejman, son of Mehmet Bey. Another note stated that, in 1921, Bukojna had 300 houses. *'There aren't even two hundred left,'* I thought. This was our village's fate; when there was food, its population increased, when there wasn't, it decreased. *'Teacher wanted to tell our story,'* I thought. This is why he visited Majka so often; she was "living history", as he'd say. 'And who is "dead history"?' I wanted to ask, but it seemed like a very haughty question and I postponed it for the following days…later…later…Never! All I could do was read what others had written about us and our Gora:

A small ethnic group, somewhat unknown, in a crisis-stricken province of Kosovo, is seeking its own identity. Recently, the correspondent of "Voice of America" for Eastern Europe, Krist Negele, visited the Gorani localities in Kosovo and sent us the following report:

'In the valley of the Sharr Mountains, beyond the border with Albania, in the south-eastern region of Kosovo, the settlements of more than 16 thousand Gorani are to be found. There are 36 large and small villages on the hilly slopes, half of them with Albanians. Almost 18 villages are inhabited only by the Gorani. They dress like Albanians, practice Islam and speak a dialect which they call "Gorani" or "*nashke*", which means "our language" in their dialect. Many of them have migrated to Turkey, even though their language is not Turkish. Many others have moved from this valley to other parts of Kosovo or even to Belgrade and Bosnia, in search of better opportunities. In most of these villages, there is no industry, and almost all Gorani women are housewives due to the lack of jobs.'

Nobody is certain about the true origins of the Gorani. 'We came from the fog,' they say, wretchedly. It is not known for sure whether they are Slavicized Albanians, Slavicized Turks, Islamised Slavs, Macedonians or Serbs. Bulgarians also claim them as their own. Meanwhile, they themselves feel like orphans. 'Orphans, but in our own home.' When someone tells them, 'you don't know what you are,' they respond saying, 'yes, but we know what we are not.'

'We don't even know how the Gorani ethnic group came to be. We have neither writers nor educated people; we have almost nothing but our sorrowful songs.'

46

Before I could even finish reading all the papers Teacher gave me, I heard that they were looking for me, but I did not answer. When I went upstairs, with my head spinning from what I had read, everyone asked me in unison, 'Where have you been?' Those days, I was asked more and more often; they seemed to be worried about me. 'In the scullery,' I responded, as that's what we called the alcove where we kept our winter goods. 'I went to see if there were any pears left from those we put in water.'

'The delegates left none.' Mother said. 'Don't even mention them,' Father added.

I sat down to eat with my brothers and sisters. It seemed to be a good day, as Mother had prepared corn pie and pickled cabbage, which I had at Mursel when I went to get grain. How I longed to sit next to that good old man, with his silky-soft beard and those small hands, which stirred the embers with tongs so that I could warm up and dry faster…But instead of the laid-back conversation of Mursel, I heard Uncle's noisy and enraged shouts:

'What have you done? What did you tell the investigators and what documents did you give them?'

The corn pie got stuck in my throat. I could barely muster a few sounds from my mouth, which was also quivering.

'What?'

Uncle looked me in the eye, stared at me for a few moments that seemed so all too long, and, then, asked Father and me to go to another room.

'What has happened?' Father asked anxiously.

'The entire province and the city are gossiping that the Teacher was reported by one of his students, to whom he had given many of the documents that the police could not find…I don't believe it was you, but…Tell us!' Uncle pushed me.

'I gave neither them nor your diary to anyone!'

'Where are they, then?'

'I hid them,' I said a little bit more confidently.

'Where?' Father asked.

'Where you hid the gold when the army occupied our house,' I said.

They were speechless. One did not believe that I knew the secrets of the diary, while the other didn't know that I had discovered the secret hole where he hid the gold.

I went downstairs to bring them all the papers, but they followed me. When we entered the scullery, I gave them the package of everything Teacher had entrusted me with…

'Now, we are all involved.' Uncle said, glancing at the letters, 'Even the Voice of America?'

'No,' said Father, 'I am alone in this, and I'll take care of these. I'm used to it. You know, I didn't hand over the rifle. I hid it and it has been years but they've not found it…'

When we went back to the kitchen, Mother was shrouded in fear and her lower jaw was trembling, hitting the upper one.

'It's nothing,' Father said and went up to the third-floor room to find a place for Teacher's papers. There must have been other holes hidden in the walls.

As if everything they said in court about me was not enough; that is, I gave the investigator Teacher's poems, one of which very dangerous—the one supposedly dedicated to a poet, but about which the "writer" who performed the analysis had determined that if the first letters of each line were vertically joined, they read: "Ballad to myself"—or those articles about Gora and the Gorani, which Teacher had taken from "Voice of America", or that Teacher had beaten a policeman to release an old woman, who had insulted the state by calling it a hell-state and a shitty state; hence, as if all these were not enough, another story spread among the people: a big fat lie. But what could one do about Bubllanka? She was a chubby woman, whose husband had fled three years ago, leaving her alone with their six children. She had been deported to Tepelena, but nobody understood why they brought her back, before even crossing Qafa e Gjarprit. Two months ago, she went to the town, and people didn't know if she had been interned there to be kept away from the border, or if she went to marry a warehouseman with a belly the size of a cabbage. She was soon forgotten about, and she would have remained in the thorns of oblivion—like rags blown by the wind—had she not been brought to testify in the trial against Teacher.

'He raped me!' she said. 'Then?' the prosecutor asked.

197

'Then he'd come to me every night and I was ashamed to tell…'

'What did he say to you?'

'He talked against the state. He said it is a shitty state, life here is worse than in hell. He said that in our village, the soldier's boot and the ignorance of the chief rule…'

'What do you have to declare, defendant?' the prosecutor asked.

'I have nothing to state, but I have only one question: Do you really think that I, a young man from Shkodra, would fall for this rotten haystack? Do not take me for the captain!'

'Listen here', the prosecutor replied, 'first, the questions are asked by me, not you; second, do not insult the witness; and third, it should be noted down that the defendant demonstrated racist tendencies, which aggravates his already compromised position.'

When the news of this testimony reached the village, the words "spy" and "traitor" that had been spread about me, started to be forgotten. Moreover, in one of the court hearings, Teacher himself had declared: 'Why do you slander my student? Everything you say is true: I have listened to the "Voice of America", and I have written that poem, the ballad to myself. But it was not my student to tell you. Why don't you mention the name of the informant, or are you sparing it to make him principal, chief or even parliament member later? You only know the title of the poem, the second title, but you don't have the text; if you have it, just show it…'

'We don't need to read your nonsense,' the prosecutor interrupted him.

Nonetheless, people distanced themselves from me, both those who were benevolent to Teacher and those who didn't like him. The first because they thought I sold him out, while the second because the state now considered me more valuable than them, who had been fawning for years over every delegate who came to the village. 'Who would have guessed? Such a snake in the grass!…Who knows why they didn't put him in jail or send him to exile along with all his kinfolk?'

47

Yet, when the news from the city reached us, the whole village seemed to shake to its core. Teacher was sentenced to execution! It no longer occurred to anyone to find the culprits of his sentence inside the village. 'This is not a matter of papers and kids; the fog has thickened and risen high.'

The earthquake that shook the human senses in that remote and unknown village altogether was followed by more news. Teacher would be executed at the Bear Scaffold! Only then did everyone notice that those logs and slats erected quickly by the soldiers on a cold, frosty morning were still there, motionless and menacing. Some even asked: 'When did they erect those cursed logs again; who put them there?'

Neither then nor today—after fifty-seven years—have I come to learn and understand what I did, what I said, what I thought, whom I spoke to and whom I didn't, whom I saw and whom I avoided. It seemed that I was living in an underground pit, in an ancient world where death had not yet been invented, and, every night, I woke up frightened by the howls of little bears. But when I opened my eyes, the stillness of the night and the neglect of the stars hurt me; the ashes of stones dried my mouth and a rope of fog around my throat suffocated me.

When they brought Teacher, he looked at the people longingly—a melancholic smile on his face—and shook his head lightly, so lightly that only those who had loved him, and still did, realised that he was greeting them. He noticed me when they put him on the bear scaffold. He looked straight into my eyes, as if to say: Never forget this day, don't forget me either…My eyes were stinging and my chest was bursting. The commands pierced through my temples like knives: 'Ready!' and then 'Fire!' After the soldiers' bullets, Teacher fell on the slats and I could only see the dripping blood…Some women started weeping and wailing; the men left, their heads hanging. I ran towards the howling that called me and roped me in towards the abyss where no white clouds were to be seen Chilam…Balam…Chumayel…The little orphaned bears were howling.

It was past midnight and I still didn't know where I was. I carelessly trampled through puddles and the muddy ground seemed even filthier than it really was...Snow is falling like soot...Death befell, but we saw each other not ... From afar, I heard people calling my name. I saw lanterns moving, whereas I had forgotten to walk. The lanterns approached, and in their light, I recognised Father, Uncle and two or three other men. Mother held my hand and pulled me gently. 'Let's go home,' she said in a weak voice. When we got home, I got a better sense of how alarmed they had been. They had been looking for me for five hours. Scared that I might have fallen from the steep cliffs of Shap, or that I might have fled across the border, or that the bears might have torn me apart... Uncle sat down next to me and handed me a piece of crumpled paper. I opened it. 'I know you did not betray me!' I recognised Teacher's handwriting.

'He handed it to me when he passed through us towards death,' Uncle said. I started weeping as Mother took my head on her lap...

Two days later, Uncle discovered where Teacher had been buried, without a mark, without anything, as if in a desert. The ground had been flattened and covered with cracks to make sure that he would never be found. 'We don't know where the great poet's bones rest,' I remembered his words. Uncle put a stone on top of the grave, and I, a bunch of Gora flowers. Days later, others heard of it, and as they passed by, they'd occasionally place a stone; thus, a wall was erected. The girls of the village—who came after two weeks—also passed solemnly by the little wall, some of them adding stones. Neither on that day nor on the following evenings did they sing songs by the seven gates of Bukojna.

One day, Majka sent for me. I knew that, since the shooting of "the Shkodra Boy", she wouldn't talk to anyone. 'Take me to him,' she told me. We left right away. From afar, I noticed that the wall's stones had disappeared; they had been scattered and thrown down the stream, and the empty pit looked like a black wound on the planet. 'They took him,' I shouted. 'Where did they take him, where did they throw him, where is he, where, where?'

'He's in the sky, he's with the stars,' Majka said. These were the last words she ever said...

Tirana, 2014

Synopsis
The Girls of Fog

A novel by Albanian writer Namik Dokle.

At the end of the world, or in the middle of nowhere, there is a small village called Bukojna. It is located in Gora, a province of Albanian inhabited by an ethnic minority called the Gorani, who speak their own unique language, tell their own legends, and follow their own rites and customs, and who are believed to be of Bogomil origins. According to the legends, in Bukojna, the sun rises twice every day and the moon sets twice every dawn. The ancient settlement has also welcomed more inhabitants of various origins, from the good-looking Vlachs and the knowledgeable Jews to the brave and proud highlanders.

It is a village where 'men of turn grey when still children and see better at night than at daylight,' as Majka, a supposedly three-hundred-year-old woman forgotten by death, says. It is precisely in this microcosm of the Albanian Gora— where the obligatory norms of a new life stipulated by the dictatorship of the proletariat try to enroot themselves with the ruthlessness and harshness that characterised the fifties—that the novel's events are narrated through the scrutinising and suspicious outlook of a child.

The effort to bring to light the suffocating and contracting existence of a community, divided, as if with a sword, between the two states of Albania and Yugoslavia ('Enver there, Tito here, fog in the middle'), also sheds light on the spiritual resistance to protect its identity, language, culture and centuries-old tradition as well as the endeavour to continue to exist and be loyal to itself, in these "new" times of repression.

The violent attempt to uproot a person's memory, their identity, turns into savageness towards everything that is human, including the ownership of the land, the use of pastures in the border area, the celebration of St George, wedding customs, Majka's prayers, the song of the girls who gather every evening at the seven gates of the village, as well as towards legends and even curses—like that of Sinan Pasha—but, first and foremost, towards reason, free speech and the solidarity represented by the Teacher and, finally, towards the incontestable human right to preserve one's dignity, as exemplified in the words: 'You either are a man or not!'

The repressive regime of Enver Hoxha grabs hold of these people and refuses to let go; everything turns to be gloomy when the young girls of the village are forced to go to action as "volunteers" in the construction of a hydropower plant and are not allowed to even come back for St George's celebrations. The land at the border no longer belongs to anybody; the basement of the communist organisation becomes something to be feared; the committee with a balcony and the one with no balcony control everything, through the border post commander, the party secretary of the village—a self-proclaimed Stalin—the political police, the spies and the plaintiffs who claim to strive "for the good of the people". The taxes and obligations that involve the handing over of agricultural products to the state bring about a regime of starvation, not reluctant to annihilate whoever seemingly disobeys, be it a bear, a white dog that "bites the new state", or the poet Teacher.

Yet that small village hidden among the mountains, from which the regime tries to take away the magic and the natural flow of life, manifests its resistance, in the only way it knows and can: in the face of the brutal and filthy tumult created by the new rulers, it stubbornly preserves its folklore and dialect, as reflected in the vivid language of the characters and the incorporated immortal songs.

In other words, this is not the story of a remote village, but one of survival and resistance, enriched with the tonalities and colours of ballads, which turn a seemingly familiar chronicle into the Saga of Gora. This first novel to focus on the Gorani is not only a fascinating story that can be read in one sitting, but also, as the well-known Bosnian academician Kulenovic underlines, it is a necessary work of art.

Namik Dokle—Albania.

A graduate of the University of Tirana, with a major in Journalism and another in Agrarian Economics, Namik Dokle (1946) worked for about 20 years in two of the most prominent Albanian newspapers of the time, both as a journalist and editor-in-chief, contributing with numerous articles in various fields. His political career began after the fall of the dictatorial regime in Albania (1990). Elected Member of the Parliament, his contributions were mainly in parliamentary diplomacy, and, for a considerable period of time, he contributed as a representative of Albania at varying international organisations and bodies, including the Council of Europe.

Dokle is the author of several collections of short stories, some of which have been incorporated in various anthologies. However, as the author of three collections with plays, he is better known as a playwright. In fact, eight of his fourteen plays have been successfully staged and performed for long periods in the theatres of the country. Dokle has also been awarded national and international prizes for some of them. Additionally, his six radio dramas have all been performed on Radio Tirana.

Fluent in Spanish and Serbo-Croatian, Dokle is also the translator of a variety of literary and academic works from these languages into Albanian. Yet, in recent years, his literary contribution has mostly been in the genre of the novel. He has already published four: *Vajzat e mjegulles* (*The Girls of Fog*), *Lulet e skajbotes* (*The Flowers of World's Edge*), *Ditet e lakuriqeve te nates* (*The Days of the Bats*), *Kolerë në kohë të dashurisë* (*Cholera in the Time of Love*). His Albanian publisher republished Dokle's novels more than once, while they have also been translated and have attained significant success in Bosnia Herzegovina. *The Girls of Fog* has also been published and enjoyed by the readership in Turkish and Bulgarian, which is also the expectation for its forthcoming publication in the Spanish language.